Mrs. (Matilda Charlotte) Houstoun

Sink or Swim?

Vol. 3

Mrs. (Matilda Charlotte) Houstoun

Sink or Swim?
Vol. 3

ISBN/EAN: 9783337053635

Printed in Europe, USA, Canada, Australia, Japan

Cover: Foto ©Andreas Hilbeck / pixelio.de

More available books at **www.hansebooks.com**

SINK OR SWIM?

A Novel.

BY THE AUTHOR OF

"RECOMMENDED TO MERCY,"

ETC.

IN THREE VOLUMES.

VOL. III.

LONDON:

TINSLEY BROTHERS, 18 CATHERINE ST. STRAND.

1868.

CONTENTS OF VOL. III.

SINK OR SWIM?

CHAPTER I.

"HE COMES TOO NEAR," ETC.

THE merrie month of May was speeding onward,
and with it — fast and furious — rattling over
stones, and dashing over impediments, ran the
fierce strong current of "London life." There
is an intoxicating influence, especially on the
inexperienced, in the rapid motion, the ever-
changing aspect of pleasure, the atmosphere redo-
lent of poisonous influences, that is breathed by
the upper ten thousand in the month of May, in
busy, half-mad London. By none was this insidious influence more perilously undergone than
by the impressionable, weak-nerved woman who,
through her own folly, considerably aided by " cir-

VOL. III.   B

cumstances over which she had no control," was
standing on the very brink of the abyss, the name
of which is " ruin."

It was now the middle of May, and during a
swiftly-passing fortnight Honor Beacham, con-
tinuing her course of semi-deception regarding her
father's condition, and entirely concealing from
the husband whom she believed to be exclusively
absorbed in his own pursuits and interests the
fact that her days and nights were spent in one
continued round of exciting pleasure, went on her
way—if not rejoicing, at least in a condition of
such delightful mental inebriation, that she found
barely sense or time enough to ask herself the
serious question, if the life which she was leading
indeed were joy.

John's answer to her letter, written under the
influence of hurt feeling, and penned by a man
utterly destitute, not only of the art to make a
thing appear the thing it is not, but of *l'éloquence
du billet* in general, was one exactly calculated to
rouse in a high-spirited nature a dormant inclina-
tion to rebel. In it there was an implied right to
command, a right solely arrogated (to Honor's
thinking) by reason of the writer's indifference to
her proceedings, and scanty appreciation of her
merits. "You will come back, I suppose,"—so
wrote the unwise man, who, on his side, had so

egregiously erred in his estimate of character,—
" you will come back when you have had enough
of London. I don't say to you, ' come home,'
for women that are made to do the thing they
don't like are, as mother says, not over and above
pleasant in a house. We are uncommon busy,
too, just now; there is painting to be done, and
the chintz to be calendered, so perhaps you are
as well out of the way of the bother."

Poor John! Could Honor have heard the
heavy sigh that broke from his full heart as he
closed the letter; could she, above all, have looked
into that heart and read its secret sorrows, she
could not have doubted of her husband's love; and
perhaps, removed from the glamour of Arthur
Vavasour's presence, from the mesmeric influence
of a passion which was becoming terribly overpower-
ing in its hourly-gathering strength, she might have
been again a happy woman in the simple fashion
and the humble sphere to which she had been
brought up. Such a " chance," however, was
not for the foolish, beautiful woman who, with
half-tender words (for, alas, it had come to that)
from her high-bred adorer lingering on her
memory, read the simple letter, which it had cost
so much pain to write, in anger and in bitterness.
Tossing it on her toilet-table with an impatient
jerk, she told herself that John did not care for

her. It was nothing to him, she said mentally, whether she stayed away or not; but as she inly spoke the words, the fingers of her little gauntleted hand—she had just returned from riding in the Park—dashed away something very like tears that had gathered on her long lashes and nothing short of the recollection that she was going in a few hours' time to dine at Richmond with Arthur Vavasour and a few other friends of her father's prevented her (for it would be dreadful to make her appearance with red eyes) from indulging in the luxury of a " good cry."

That party to London's prettiest suburb—an evening's enjoyment which was to include a row towards Twickenham and Teddington on the clear, flowing river, and a delicious dinner after dusk in one of the charming *cabinet particuliers* appertaining to the Star and Garter, and opening on its pleasant gardens, had been for days looked forward to with keen anticipations of delight by Honor Beacham. They were to proceed thither in two open " *hired* carriages," in one of which was to be seated Honor and the Colonel's wife, while Arthur Vavasour and a dull, unobservant Mr. Foley, a gentleman, like Pope's women, " with no character at all," were to occupy the opposite seats. In the second carriage the party collected was likely to be of a far more noisy, as well as a

more congenial, description. Mrs. Foley—a lady a
little on the wrong side of thirty, and whose animal spirits, being apt occasionally, as the saying is,
to " get the better of her," were in their full swing
of triumph on such an occasion as a Richmond
dinner—arrived at Stanwick-street punctually as
the clock struck four, arrayed in a toilet which,
but for the still more amazing costume of the
young lady with whom she was accompanied,
would have decidedly monopolised the attention
and wonder of every female observer in that quiet
neighbourhood. Shaking themselves clear of the
straw and *tumble*, consequent on their cab-drive
from some distant locality, Mrs. Foley and her
bright-eyed sister Dora Tibbets stood on the door-
steps of No. 14, laughing noisily—more noisily
than ladies of their stamp often laugh when no
one of the male sex is present to stir their spirits
up to boiling point. Their dresses, as they stood
there in the bright sunshine of a May afternoon,
were of the kind better suited to a wedding breakfast than to a " quiet dinner," as Fred Norcott
had described it, in the country. Light and fair
and frolicsome they looked; women with more
auburn frizzled hair about their heads than could,
by the most lively and charitable imagination,
have been supposed to be their own, with bright
pink roses mingling with their hirsute ornaments,

and with a *quantum suff.* of *poudre de riz* softening
the lustre of their complexions.

"How smart they are!" Honor whispered in
dismay to Arthur, as the two caught a glimpse of
the lively sisters from behind the muslin curtain of
the first-front drawing-room.

"Awfully. It's a bore they're coming, but if
there had been nobody it would have been worse,"
said Arthur, leaning over her chair, and speaking
in the low tones which always went so thrillingly
to her heart. "Imagine! I *might* have been un-
able, all this evening, to say one word alone to
you. And we have so few more days, Honor!
You say that you cannot expect a much longer
holiday; but tell me—do you never, never think
what will become of me when you are gone?"

"Don't talk in that way," she said, one of her
crimson blushes speaking far more eloquently than
her words, while she tried to hide her confusion
by carefully drawing on finger after finger of her
delicate Paris gloves. "Don't talk in that way;
I must talk to these people now. You don't know
them, of course?" And rising gracefully, she
went through the ceremony of introduction which
her father deemed it necessary to perform.

The next arrivals (they dashed up to the door
in a hansom, and remained talking up to the
balcony during the few minutes that elapsed before

the descent of the major portion of the party) were
Mr. Foley, and a young gentleman of slightly
horsey appearance, but who, nevertheless, contrived
to snip his words and lisp as ridiculously as any
foolish would-be fine gentleman in town.   Captain
Bowles was the son of a general officer, and was
himself, though of small dimensions, and of anything but military bearing, a soldier.   He was
plain of feature, with a large mouth and a beardless face.   His appearance was more that of an
inferior order of counter-jumper than of a guards-
man; nevertheless he was petted and made much
of, especially by the fair sex.   Mrs. Foley and her
sister were " fine women," and " fast," so the
general's son—who would have been voted, under
less favourable circumstances, a little snob—was
allowed to stand up before them with his hands in
his trousers pockets like a man; and while he
minced his platitudes with graceful ease, was
smiled on as fondly as though he were a hero and
a gentleman.

   There could scarcely have been found a more
good-natured *chaperone, duenna,*—call her what
you will,—than the Colonel's lanky wife, seated
opposite to dull, sleepy Mr. Foley, who, by the
way, was an individual of no particular profession,
gaining a precarious livelihood as " director" to
one or two doubtful companies, and having a float-

ing capital in the same. Mrs. Norcott, under cover of her pink parasol, kept up a dozy conversation with that harmless man of business, while Arthur Vavasour, who had no right whatever (seeing that his young wife was in the most delicate of situations—nervous during his absence, and only comforted by the certainty that he was within call) to be there at all, had—alas for the credit of poor selfish human nature!—forgotten every duty, and ignored the sacred claims of wifehood, for the sake of passing a few blissful hours by the side of the forbidden woman he adored. And she—that other wife, who still, strange as it may seem, and eke impossible to many, kept a large corner in her heart for home and duty, and the rough, tender-hearted man she called her husband—what were her thoughts, her feelings, as the tempter, with his bold beseeching eyes fixed on her blushing face, told her, in looks more dangerous still than words, the bewildering, but as yet only half-welcome truth that she was all the world to him, and that, to gain her love, he would cast to the four winds of heaven every tie on earth, as well as every hope of heaven?

For it had come to that with this "fond, foolish," passionate young man. Made of the stuff that loves in wild extremes, unused to put a bridle on his fierce desires, restrained by no sweet early home-affections, the dear love, mother-love, that bids the profligate, sometimes in his wildest moments, to go no further—only a myth to him—with a God above but half believed in, and himself the deity on earth he worshipped—who can wonder that this man, vigorous with the strength and health of his one-and-twenty years, should make no effort to resist the devil that, without resistance, *would* not flee from him?

" How glad I am that you remembered the Park," Honor said, as they, the carriages following at a foot's pace, sauntered slowly along the beautiful wooded brow beyond Pembroke Lodge; " I would not have missed this view for the world."

They were together now,—those two who had been better far had the wide seas divided them—those two who could not but have owned that so it was, had any put the question to them in the rare sober moments which nineteen and twenty-one, in the heyday of folly and of love, are blessed with. The rest had strolled away in pairs; so that Arthur could speak as well as look his love into the bewildering eyes of his friend's lovely wife.

" Mad,—yes, I suppose I am mad," he said, in answer to a half-reproach from his companion; "but who, I ask, would not be mad—mad as you are beautiful—seeing you as I do, Honor, nearly every day, every hour? It is my fate—for by the heaven above me I *cannot* help it—to look upon your beautiful face, and see you smile, my love, my darling! Ah, do not, for the love of all that is good and beautiful, be angry with me! From the moment that I saw you first, Honor, I felt as I never felt before for mortal woman—I—"

"Don't say so. All men say that," put in Honor, who was more versed in the theory of love-making than its practice, and who, while she felt the necessity of checking her admirer's outpourings, was terribly shy and untutored in the process. "Besides, Mr. Vavasour,"—gathering courage as she proceeded,—"it is very wicked—*terribly* wicked, both for you to talk and for me to listen to such words. There is your wife at home, poor thing,—I often think of her,—how unhappy she would be could she only guess that you said such things to any woman as I have just been wicked enough to listen to!"

Arthur could scarcely repress a sigh as the image of poor neglected Sophy, stretched on her luxurious couch in the gorgeously-furnished back drawing-room in Hyde-park-terrace, presented itself to his mind's eye. "She knows nothing, guesses nothing," he said, with an ineffectual effort at carelessness. "Where ignorance is bliss, you know, it's worse than folly to be wise. I suspect there is a Bluebeard's closet in almost every house, and as long as women don't try to look inside, all goes on smoothly."

For a moment, whilst Arthur was imparting to his fair companion this result of his worldly experience, *her* thoughts glanced back to her own home, and to the marked exception to her lover's rule which it afforded. At the Paddocks—and well did Honor know that so it was—there could be found no hidden chamber barred off from the investigations of the curious. The wife of true-hearted John Beacham could pry at her own wondering will into any and every corner of his big warm heart, and find there no skeleton of the past, no flesh-covered denizen of the present, warning her with uplifted finger that he was false.

Very guilty she felt for a second or two, and humbled and odious, as the consciousness of being a vile deceiver sent a blush to her fair cheek, and checked any answering words that had risen to her tongue. Time, however, for useful reflection was denied her. The sound of her father's voice announcing that it was five o'clock, and that the boats were waiting at the Castle-stairs, effectually interrupted a reverie of a more wholesome description than might, under the circumstances, have been expected; and, reëntering their respective carriages, the party were soon on their way down the hill so loved by Cockney pleasure-seekers, and so be sung by nature-worshipping poets.

Once in the large comfortable wherry which had been hired for the occasion, Arthur found very little opportunity, beyond that of paying the most devoted attention to her personal comfort, of making himself agreeable to his lady-love. That there was *one* subject, at least, besides herself of real and almost absorbing interest to Arthur Vavasour soon became evident to Honor; and that subject was the approaching Derby race. Since her instalment in Stanwick-street, Honor had heard more talk of that all-important annual event than—horse-breeder's wife though she was—she had listened to through all the many months of her married life; and naturally enough, seeing that the "favourite" was her father's property, and that Arthur Vavasour appeared deeply interested in the triumph of Rough Diamond, the success of that distinguished animal became one of the most anxious wishes of Mrs. John Beacham's heart.

"O, I do so hope he'll win!" she exclaimed enthusiastically; "he is such a wonderfully beautiful creature. And he has a brother who, they think, will be more perfect still;—no, not a brother quite, a half-brother, I think he is; and I used to watch him every day led out to exercise, looking

so wild and lovely. He is only a year old, and
his name is Faust; and they say he is quite sure
to be a Derby horse."

Poor Honor! In her eagerness on the subject,
and her intense love of the animal whose varied
charms and excellences were to be seen in such
perfection in her husband's home, she had been
inadvertently "talking shop" for the amusement
of the spurious fine ladies, whose supercilious
glances at each other were not, even by such a
novice as Honor Beacham, to be mistaken. In
a moment—for the poison of such glances is as
rapid as it is insidious—two evil spirits, the spirits
of anger and of a keen desire to be avenged, took
possession of our heroine. She saw herself despised, and—so true is it that we cannot scarcely
commit the smallest sin without doing an injury
as well to our neighbours as to ourselves—she
resolved, to the utter extinction of the very inferior beauties near her, to make the most of the
wondrous gift of loveliness which she was conscious of possessing. Hitherto she had "borne
her faculties meekly;" the consciousness that she
was, by marriage, without the pale of the "upper
ten thousand" had, together with an innate modesty which was one of her rarest charms, kept
her silent and somewhat subdued when in what
is called "company." It had required the looks

of contempt which she had seen passing between
the well-got-up sisters to rouse the spirit of display
in Honor Beacham's heart; but, once aroused,
the intoxication of success encouraged her to proceed, and the demon of Coquetry was found hard
indeed to crush.

The row, slow and dreamy, up-stream to Ted-
dington-lock, would, even had there been no un-
lawful and much-prized lover—of whom, explain it
as you will, Honor was more than half afraid—by
her side, have been simply delightful. The river
was so purely clear that the water-weeds beneath
its pellucid surface showed brightly, freshly green;
and then the long low islets, with the graceful
willow-boughs, vivid with the hues of early spring,
dipping their last-opened buds into the laving
stream, and the banks, verdant and fair, and
cattle-sprinkled—all combined to make a Breughal-
like picture of spring verdure and beauty.

Notwithstanding a certain amount of horsey
conversation, flirting, covert as well as open, was
the order of the afternoon. Both Mrs. Foley and
her sister were adepts at that truly feminine and
easily-acquired accomplishment. To look the
thing they meant not, to understand or not understand the ingenious *double entendre*, to give the
little hope that hinders from despair, and *only* the
little hope, lest the excited lover should presume,

were arts in which *ces dames*, the unprofessional
demi-monde of gay middle life, were thoroughly
skilled.   It required more audacity than Honor
would have previously believed that she possessed
to cope with rivals such as these, but, *champagne
aidant*, she got through the female duty well;
and the dinner which succeeded the aquatic ex-
cursion owed not a little of its success to the lively
spirits lending added charms to the powerful influence of beauty.

The hour of ten had struck by the town clocks,
and the many wine-bottles on the table of No. 3
room were near to emptying, before it occurred to
any of the party therein assembled that the night
was fine and warm and starlight, and that in the
gardens of the hotel a fresher, purer air could be
imbibed than that which reminded them somewhat
too forcibly of the good things they had been im-
bibing.

At a conjugal hint from the Colonel, his watchful and obedient wife suggested that the moon
had risen, and was looking lovely over the river.
A turn on the terrace would be delightful, she
thought; and as her proposal met with no opposition, they made themselves an impromptu
drawing-room under the starry canopy of heaven.

" What a lovely night! how glad I am to

have seen this! The moonlight never looked to me so soft and beautiful before!"

"Never? I am glad of that," Arthur said, his face very near to Honor's as they leant over the stone balustrade and gazed out upon the tranquil scene. "I may hope then that, for a little while at least, the memory of this night will linger with you. It is a day that I at least shall find it very hard to forget. You smile and shake your head. Perhaps you take me for one who knows nothing of his own mind,—one whom a fresh face can stir into new and soon-to-be-changed feelings. But, Honor, listen to me—listen while we have these few moments we can call our own. I tell you that the love I feel for you is one that will defy all time and space and change. You have never been loved, my beautiful one, with such a love as this. You would tell me, were you not an angel, and too pure and good for such a world as this, that your husband—"

"Hush, hush! please don't; I cannot bear to hear you speak of him, Mr. Vavasour,—well, well, _Arthur_—I know I have been very weak and wicked; but for my own folly you would never have—have told me that you loved me; and indeed I did not mean—I—"

He seized both her little hands in his strong grasp, and held them there as in a vice.

"Honor," he whispered,—and his voice trembled with concentrated passion,—"are you going to tell me that I have been a blundering fool, and that I have mistaken every look and word and smile that led me on to love you? If so,—but no, I cannot, will not think it possible. Long ago, my darling,"—and his voice softened into entreaty,—"long ago, when first I held this precious hand in mine, you might, with cold words and scanty smiles, have taught me"—and he smiled bitterly—"my place. But that you did not do, Honor: you *know* you did not. What your motive was in leading me on to hope that I was something—a very little—more to you than a mere acquaintance, you best can say. If it were well meant on your part, all I can say is that it was cruel kindness; for it will be a hard fall down again to the place from which your gentle words and smiles had raised me. But once more, Honor, for the love of Heaven, tell me that you have not trifled with me. Do not make me lose my faith in every woman. Tell me before we part to-night that if we were doomed never to meet again you would sorrow a little, just a very little, for my loss. Tell me that sometimes, when you are alone, you think of me; tell me"—and he ventured unreproved to steal his arm round her waist—"tell me that you love me just a very little, Honor, in

return for the heart's whole devotion that I feel
for you."

Her bosom heaved, and her heart beat very
quickly, under the strong firm pressure of his
hand; but for all that—and perhaps some of my
readers may understand the anomaly—the strongest
feeling in Honor Beacham's mind at that important crisis was one of relief that she was not
alone with her adorer. And yet in one sense she
loved him. His touch, his lingering gaze into
the depths of her blue eyes, exercised—and never
more so than at that moment—a strange magnetic
influence over her nerves. She could ill have
borne a decree that banished Arthur Vavasour
from her society, and yet she felt that he was to
play no actual part in the misty future of her life
—the life which she never doubted she was to
spend with John; the life that *might* be a tolerably happy one when Mrs. Beacham was gathered
—not to her forefathers, but to the place allotted
to her by her dead husband's side.

Honor, to do her justice, never imagined an
existence apart from her husband. She was not
happy at home; the life there was unsuited to her,
and John, she believed, did not love her well
enough to care whether his mother tormented
her or not. In London, on the contrary, she *did*
enjoy herself, wildly, feverishly, but with a zest and

an impulse that had nothing in it that was natural
or lasting. When the day came, she longed for
the hour which should bring Arthur Vavasour to
her side; but with the longing came a kind of
nervous dread—a fear of his impatience, an alarm
as of a hunted animal at the thought of finding
herself within his power—all which symptoms
might have told a more experienced woman that
in her love for Arthur Vavasour there was an
alloy which, had he imagined its existence, would
have deprived the longing for possession of more
than half its value.

It is often a misfortune to all parties concerned
that the same symptoms are indicative of various
and opposite complaints. A blush is as often a
sign of innocence as of guilt; and a beating heart
beneath a *visibly* agitated bosom may be a token
of other emotions besides the tender one of love.

When Arthur felt the throbbing pulse bound-
ing beneath the pressure of his hand, he never
doubted that, had he been *tête-à-tête* with that
most peerless creature, she would have gladly sighed
her love out on his breast, listening in tender
ecstasy to his vows of eternal constancy. Nearer
and nearer, happy in this blessed conviction, to his
heart he held her, secured from observation in a
shadowy corner, and *safe* under the protection of

the remainder of the party, who lingered just out of earshot on the terrace.

Honor, afraid of offending her high-born lover, and sincerely hoping that never—*never* under less safe and satisfactory circumstances might a similar scene be enacted, contrived to stammer out the foolish, false, and guilty assurance,—an assurance that filled the young lover's heart with the wildest hopes—the assurance, namely, that her heart was his, and that in his love she found her dearest, sweetest happiness!

CHAPTER II.

A LOVER FOUND AND LOST.

" I REALLY am at a loss to make up my mind
which is the most extraordinary—the man behaving in this way without encouragement, or your
being so lost to everything that is—ahem !—due to
your position in life as to allow him to think, to
hope, that his proposals—*most* impertinent ones,
I must say—*could* meet with anything but anger
and contempt."

Lady Millicent was seated on her presidential
sofa, in the room appropriated in Bolton-square to
her especial use. It was a dull, dark, business-
looking apartment. The " third drawing-room " it
was called, and in it milady was wont to receive
such visitors as clearly were not there for purposes
of mere pleasure, or with the intention of epheme-
rally enjoying themselves — men of law, serious
men, with faces fraught with the care that the
craving after six-and-eightpences is wont to im-
press on the human countenance divine, were

seen entering, clearly with a purpose, the heavy door (white-painted and gilt, but shabby and tarnished now) that led to milady's sanctum. It was a room into which her young daughters rarely intruded; and when, on the morning in question (it was that of the very day which Honor passed so feverishly with Arthur Vavasour by her side), Rhoda, poor, timid, nervous Rhoda, was summoned to an audience with her awe-inspiring mamma, she made her *entrée* with a beating heart, and, though she knew not wherefore, with a strong presentment of evil. The open letter in Lady Millicent's hand was scarcely evidence enough to awaken in her mind anything at all approaching to the truth. Rhoda was as far as the poles from imagining that the sedate rector of Switcham, the quiet, unpretending young man, whose "duties" ever seemed so much above his pleasures, could have so far allowed his mundane feelings, his passions, that were of the "earth, earthy," to overpower his well-regulated mind, as to induce him to offer to the great lady of Gillingham—the patroness of his living, and one with whom he knew himself to be *not* a favourite—his humble proposals for her daughter's hand.

Standing droopingly in the august presence, and without a word to say either in her own behalf or that of her co-delinquent, the poor girl listened in silence to the stern and very bitter words of reprobation which fell from her mother's lips. Perhaps until she so listened—until she contrasted the hard unsympathising nature of the woman to whom she owed her birth with that of the good, thoroughly-to-be-relied-on character of the man whose letter, with dimmed eyes and a very pitying heart, she had just contrived to read and comprehend—she had never rightly known how necessary the love of him, who for so many months had been her only object and point of interest at uncongenial Gillingham, had become to her.

"I am well aware—no justly-reproachful words of yours can make me more so" (thus one sentence of poor George's letter ran)—"that I have no right, in a worldly point of view, to hope that you would look otherwise than contemptuously on my humble offer. I have little besides my deep affection, and my prayers that God would enable me to contribute to your beloved daughter's happiness, to lay before one who deserves every good gift that could be bestowed upon her. A small, *very* small private fortune—a few hundreds a year only—in addition to the income derived from my living, is all that I possess. But, if I mistake not, Miss Vavasour's tastes are simple ones, and she *might*, God aiding, be happier in the quiet home

which she would deign to share with me than in
the turmoil of the great world, and amongst the
gay and rich, of whom it is said that it is hard for
them to enter the kingdom of heaven."

"Methodistical stuff!" murmured Lady Millicent, turning over the leaves of a law-book, and
delivering herself of the severe comment on her
would-be son-in-law's epistle at the moment when
she rightly guessed that poor Rhoda had arrived
at its conclusion. "Very bad taste, I think, my
dear, of your admirer, condemning us *en masse* in
this summary way. But now, *do* tell me," laying
down the pen with which she had been making
notes, "what *did* you do at Gillingham to bring
upon me such a letter as that? I should have
thought—but one lives and learns—that if there
existed a girl in the world who would have ab-
stained from this kind of thing, it was you; and
now I find that—"

"O, mamma!" began poor Rhoda, whose
delicacy (and she was sensitively delicate) was severely wounded by this exordium,—"O, mamma,
I did nothing! Indeed, indeed, I gave no—I
mean—I did not lead—"

And then she stopped, poor girl, from utter
inability to make herself understood by the parent
whose cold unwomanly eyes were fixed with such
unassisting scrutiny on her blushing face. There

are mothers and mothers, even as (I was about to say) there are friends and friends: but in using such a conjunction I was wrong, for of that rare hypostasis there can be but one variety; degrees of comparison exist not in that particular noun substantive of the many which signify " to be, to do, and to suffer." Either a friend's love passeth the love of woman, and he sticketh closer than a brother, or he is that daily-met-with and more generally-useful thing, *id est*, a good-natured acquaintance, whose services, should they not chance to interfere with his own requirements, may possibly be at our disposal. But to return to Rhoda Vavasour's natural friend—to the one being who had it in her power, and whose sacred duty it was, as far as mortal skill can do the heavenly work, to make the crooked straight and the rough places plain to the weaker and the tottering vessel, who was less able than herself to bear the burden and the heat of the day. A few words softly, wisely spoken, a kind caress, the sweet conviction, in some unknown mysterious way conveyed, that she, the mother, was the best, the most heaven-deputed guardian for her child, would have convinced that child, whose experience of life was *nil,* and who had seen no man save her brothers whom she could compare with the right-minded young rector of Switcham, that an engagement with that reverend gentleman might

not be exactly a desirable consummation, or one,
save by the good man himself, prudently as well as
devoutly to be wished. Rhoda was a girl thoroughly
amenable to reason, as well as one whom the silken
cords of affection could have led with the lightest,
tenderest touch. Delicate of frame, physically as
well as mentally, she could ill bear the wear and
tear of either excitement or worry; and perhaps
George Wallingford had said no more than the
truth when he suggested that her life, in the seclu-
sion of a country parsonage, would probably pass
more happily away than were the nervous girl to
be thrown into the whirlpool of stir and fashion,
there to be tossed to and fro amongst the vessels
of iron, against which her frailer, humbler self
would be hopelessly, maybe, bruised and broken.

To convince Lady Millicent of this truth would,
however, have required eloquence far greater than
that possessed by the lowly-born clergyman, who
certainly had not chosen the very likeliest way in
the world to gain his ends. As milady had truly
said, there were but two ways of accounting for
the reverend gentleman's preposterous conduct,
and neither of those two ways was calculated to
throw a roseate hue over the matter. That Rhoda
— her favourite, because her most submissive,
daughter—had degraded herself to the degree of
giving encouragement to "the man" for whose

audacity no words were sufficiently severe, caused
as much surprise and indignation to the magnifi-
cent widow as if she had systematically and kindly
encouraged her child to pour out into the maternal
breast her cares, her sorrows, and her joys.   That
a heart, young and love-requiring, will, in default
of home aliment, seek elsewhere for its natural,
and in some cases even necessary, food, this
mother, engrossed by her own plans and projects for personal aggrandisement and power, had
never yet suspected.   Lady Millicent—a stay-at-
home, " domestic" woman, a " widow indeed,"
and one of those constitutionally prudent matrons
against whom the tongue of scandal never had for
a single instant wagged —was precisely one of
those individuals with whom self-deception is the
very easiest thing in life.   Her hopes and wishes,
her thoughts and fancies, never—that she could
truly have said — soared above or beyond the
boundaries of her own property ; and the interests of her children, she had taught herself to
believe, were the groundwork and the motive
power of all the hard, unwomanly business that
she had set herself to do.

"You are not aware, perhaps," she said coldly
to the poor girl who stood unconsciously doubling
down and plaiting with her trembling fingers the
fringe of the table-cover that hung near her,—

"you are not aware, I daresay, that, unless I succeed—for the benefit of my younger children—in a law-suit which is in progress, your fortune, as well as Katherine's, will be very trifling indeed. Had your poor father lived, there would, of course, have been an opportunity of remedying this evil, this *injustice*," she added firmly, and with a stress upon the word which poor Rhoda was far too much engrossed by her own troubles to notice. "I tell you this, not that you may suppose that, under *any* circumstances, you could have been permitted to disgrace your family by marrying this extraordinarily presumptuous person, but because I wish you to understand that a *good* marriage may be positively necessary, both for you and for Katherine. By the way, now that we are on this disagreeable subject, will you allow me to ask whether she—whether your sister, who seems to me to be self-willed and forward enough for anything—knew of this—this disgraceful entanglement : for entanglement, Rhoda," she went on severely, "there must have been. Poor as my opinion naturally is of the intellect of a person who could write such a letter as that" (pointing to it contemptuously), "quoting Scripture too in such a personal and impertinent manner, still I cannot believe that the man *could* have been such an egregious fool, could have been so propos-

terously silly, as to have written to me, if you—
just look at me, will you, instead of at the carpet
—had not said or done something to authorise his
presumption."

The cold eyes fixed upon the now tearful face
before her seemed to command as well as to expect an answer. None, however, came; so, still
more authoritatively, Lady Millicent—could she
find no better way of improving her talents (*id
est*, her children) and of showing her appreciation
of the legacy committed to her charge, than by
thus torturing the feelings of Cecil Vavasour's
young daughter?—Lady Millicent pressed the
question to which she had hitherto received none
but the least comprehensible of replies.

"Answer me. Really I have no more time to
waste. Had you any idea that this Mr. Wallingford intended making the application which strikes
me as so extraordinary?"

With some difficulty, Rhoda managed to stammer forth a negative. "Indeed no," she said;
"and, mamma, Kate knew no more about it than
I did. I never told her—I mean, I—"

She stopped suddenly, her face the colour of
the setting sun when, "cradled in vermilion," it
throws its red reflection over slope and mountain,
land and river. On her cheek and brow and
slender neck the tell-tale witness rushed; and

Lady Millicent—well aware that her guileless
daughter knew and felt that she had committed
herself—said, even more coldly than before:

"You are a poor dissembler, Rhoda. You
may go to your room now. Of course you allowed this man, this hypocritical *good* clergyman,
to lead you into deception. You let him fancy—
for it *is* only fancy on your part—that—"

"O mamma,—dear mamma," the girl cried
in an agony of shame and grief, "if you would
only listen to me,—only believe that I never did,
never could have done all you say! I wish I could
tell you how it was; and yet it seems—indeed it
does—as if I had nothing—*nothing* really to tell.
We used to meet—Mr. Wallingford and I—sometimes at the school, and at the poor people's cot-
tages. He is so good, mamma," gaining a little
courage when she found herself listened to without rebuke. "If you could but know how much
the sick and the old think of him, and all he does
for them, you would not wonder at—"

"At his doing one of the most unprincipled
acts of which a man can be capable," sneered Lady
Millicent. "He was perfectly well aware—he says
so in his letter—that I should be intensely angry
at his presumption; and yet—really, Rhoda, I
have no patience with your folly and wronghead-

edness—you stand up for this priggish, formal, underhand—"

"But he has not been underhand, mamma. As Mr. Wallingford is not here to tell you so himself, *I* must say the truth; and that is, that never till the day before we left Gillingham did he say one word that you might not have heard, and then he only"—and the colour deepened on her cheek—"said that he should miss me—should think of me till I came back, and that he hoped I would not quite forget Gillingham and—and 'good things' while I was away."

Lady Millicent laughed scornfully.

"For Gillingham read Mr. Wallingford, and for good things the delights, I suppose, of Switcham Parsonage,—boiled leg of mutton and what is called, I believe, a parlour-maid to wait upon you. My dear Rhoda, be thankful that such a fate as becoming the wife of a poor country parson is not in store for you. And now, my dear, you may go, as I said before, to your own room. There is no occasion to make this sort of thing public. *I* shall of course answer Mr. Wallingford's letter, and I think I may venture to say that we are not likely to be troubled further on the subject. There, there, that will do; I am very much engaged this morning,"—arresting the words which she could see were hovering on her daughter's lips,—"and I can afford to waste no more time on such nonsense as this."

The head and eyes resolutely bent upon the folio before her, the decided tone of a voice whose stern, determined accents Rhoda knew and understood full well, convinced the timid girl that appeal there was none, and that nothing remained for her but to obey. With a heavy heart she ascended the stairs to the chamber that she called her own, and which, opening into a smaller one appropriated to Kate, enabled that lighter-spirited young lady to overhear through the keyhole of the door the hardly suppressed sobs which broke from the breast of the unhappy Rhoda.

"My darling, what *is* the matter?" cried the younger girl, rushing in impetuously,—for Kate's strong points were certainly neither prudence nor self-control, — "what is the matter, you poor dear?" And tumbling on her knees by the side of her weeping sister, Kate began sobbing too by sheer force of sympathy.

A very few words sufficed to put the latter *au fait* of the secret—*secret,* alas, no longer—which Rhoda had so long and so sedulously kept. Kate listened with eager ears and widely-distended eyes to the details, stammered forth incoherently, of this first love episode in the family. *As* a love affair, it was certainly not without its interest; but with that interest, and in spite of her sisterly compassion, Katie certainly did feel a little surprise at the singularity of Rhoda's choice. She made no allowance for the utter absence of competitors for her sister's favour; all that was patent to this damsel of fast proclivities—who thought Sunday-schools a bore, and who hoped some day to be wooed by a lover of a widely different type—was the fact that Mr. Wallingford had straight hair, was anything but "jolly," had the misfortune to possess scanty whiskers, did not smoke, and, to sum up all his defects in one comprehensive word, was a "parson."

"I can't the least understand how Rhoda can *care* for him," she said an hour afterwards to her eldest brother, to whom she had just narrated the provoking circumstance that her sister, who was in love with that stupid Mr. Wallingford, had cried so long and so bitterly that she wasn't fit to be seen,—"a man who is always talking ' good,' and who, of course, thinks it's wicked to be jolly. Can you make it out, Arthur? I suppose it was all done by staring at each other, for *I* never saw them speaking, or seeming as if anything was going on."

"Of course you didn't," her brother said, as he settled his cravat in the pier-glass over the mantelshelf (he was going to ride—his usual morn-

ing avocation—with Honor Beacham, and naturally wished to look his best on the occasion),—"of
course you didn't. Girls when they are in love
(and the best girls too) will deceive even other
women,—a very different affair, I can tell you,
from taking in a man; and if you think, my dear
Katie—"

"O don't bother about that now," Kate said
impatiently. "I asked you whether you *can* believe that Rhoda really likes Mr. Wallingford. *I*
can't fancy his being a lover : horrid creature, I
call him! Now, Arthur, do attend one moment.
I want to know whether I ought to be glad or
sorry that mamma has put an end to the business,
and—"

"Glad, to be sure," said Arthur, taking up
his gloves, and troubling himself less than was
altogether brotherly about poor Rhoda's first and,
as the preoccupied young man considered, thoroughly uninteresting love-affair,—"glad! Why
it's the most disgusting piece of folly I ever heard
of. Such bad taste too! But it's all my mother's
fault. If a gushing young woman like Rhoda
had seen some good-looking young fellows every
now and then, she would never have got spooney
on such a slow prig of a parson as George Wallingford. An excellent young man, I daresay, in his
way; but excellent young men haven't much of

a pull in these days, except when girls haven't anyone else to talk to. Trust me, it won't be long, if I know anything about such matters, before Miss Rhoda finds another lover ready to knock this spooney fellow out of her head." And Arthur Vavasour, satisfied with this summary settlement of a question which probably appeared to him in the light of a very commonplace affair indeed, hurried away to his appointment in Stanwick-street—hurried to the presence of the still pure-hearted woman, for the love of whose bright eyes the silly young man was ready to lose his all of peace on earth, the goodwill of friends and kindred, and that much-prized but unexplainable thing for which no other nation save our own can boast even the simple name—the name, that is, of Respectability.

CHAPTER III.

WHAT WAS HONOR DOING?

IT was Sunday at the Paddocks,—Sunday afternoon,—rather a ponderous season in the old silent
house; and John was, sooth to say, a trifle tired
of his own thoughts, to say nothing of the sight of
his respectable parent poring, spectacles on nose,
over the heavy sermon (a Sabbath duty with her,
and a habit which she was far too old to break),
that kept her in a blissful doze through two hours
at least of that long afternoon of rest.

The early dinner was over; and the house
being very quiet—no sound more startling than
the buzz of the flies upon the window-pane
breaking the stillness of the restful time—John
Beacham, who had ensconced himself in his big
arm-chair, feeling dull enough, poor fellow, without Honor, began to experience not only the influence of the heat but of the Sabbath beef and
pudding; and his eyelids, "drawing straws," as
the saying is, closed gradually over the tranquil

scenes before him, and the deserted husband found himself in the land of dreams.

How long he had slept he knew not, when he was roused by a man's step in the entrance-hall near him, and by a voice which in the first bewilderment of waking he failed to recognise as that of Jack Winthrop, the owner of the wicked chestnut, and a distant neighbour, whose visits, few and far between, were usually paid on that *dies non* to a business man, a Sunday afternoon.

"Hallo, old fellow! taking a snooze, eh?" was Jack's jovial greeting; and then the two men shook hands, while Mrs. Beacham, adjusting her spectacles, and with rather a scared look in her sharp old eyes, endeavoured, under the appearance of being still more wideawake than usual, to hide the fact that she had been asleep.

Jack was not much—as he often remarked himself—of a ladies' man. He was far more at home in the stable than the drawing-room. Nevertheless, and especially when he had on his go-to-meeting coat and hat, he could shuffle through the usual forms of social good breeding with tolerable success. Of these forms, a short dissertation on the weather, past, present, and to come, together with a few polite inquiries regarding the health and whereabouts of the members of their respective families, stood first in importance. It

was to the last of these conversational duties that
Mrs. Beacham was indebted for some valuable information regarding the proceedings of the erratic
young woman whose continued absence was to the
old lady a perpetual source of mingled anger and
satisfaction.

"Well, and how do you get along without the
missus; eh, John?" asked the visitor. And then,
with a rather meaning wink and a jerk of his
smoothly-brushed yellow head, "I expect I've
seen Mrs. John since you have; caught sight of
her yesterday morning as I was tooling through
the Park. She was a-horseback, looking like
paint,—so she was, with such a colour,—and the
young Squire along with her. There was a servant behind 'em on a screwed bay horse; and I
didn't think much of the one the missus rode
either—a leggy brute! She wouldn't think much
of him, I fancy, after Lady Meg. But you'll
have her—the missus, I mean—back again soon,
I doubt." And the worthy, stupid fellow—stupid,
that is, in everything but what regarded horse-
flesh—pulled up at last, entirely unconscious that
he had applied the match to a train, and that a
"blowing-up" of some kind or other would be
the inevitable consequence of his thoughtlessly-
spoken words.

It was not till some hours later, and when Jack

—who had been walked over every acre of the
Paddocks, and been encouraged to linger longer
than visitor had ever lingered before in each loose
box and stall—that John Beacham and his mother,
each in their several elbow-chairs, consumed their
meal of herbs—*id est,* their tea and bread-and-butter—in silence and in gloom.   John had delayed,
with a cowardice very unusual to his open, natural, fearless character, the moment, dreaded
beyond any previous moment of his life,—*that,*
namely, when Honor's conduct, her duplicity,
her shamelessness, and worst of all, her dislike
to him and to her home, would infallibly come
under discussion between himself and his mother.
To describe John's sensations during the revelations of Mr. Winthrop would be impossible.   To
hear that *his* Honor,—the fair young wife whom
he had pictured to himself living a secluded life
in her father's dull and poverty-stricken home,—
to hear, I say, from authority undeniable, that she
was recreating herself with horse exercise in the
Lady's Mile with a young gentleman,—*the* young
gentleman of whose designs, or rather the report
of whose designs, upon his wife's affections, Mrs.
Beacham had already more than once irritated
him by hinting at,—was to receive a stab sharp
and cruel, as it was wholly unexpected, in the warm
honest heart that still contained within it such a

wealth of love for the backsliding absent one.   He
had made no sign—it was his way (a misfortune
in some cases) to make no sign till such time as
the gathering stream of passion, defying all control, burst through its bonds, and spent itself in
outward fury—he made no sign of what he was
enduring whilst Honor's sin of *suppressio veri* (to
use the mildest term) was shown up in glaring
colours by his officious visitor.   From his manner
—but then Jack was not an observant character,—
that sporting individual would never have imagined
that his old friend was undergoing torture very
difficult to endure with outward composure; and
that John Beacham did so endure it was partly
owing to his dread that the old lady, who was not
famous for concealing what she called her " feelings," might, by an outburst of indignation, betray the mortifying fact that his young wife was
wronging and deceiving him.   That such a mani-
festation was to the last degree unadvisable was
so clearly and intentionally demonstrated by John's
demeanour, that Mrs. Beacham, though sorely
against her will, limited the expression of her
wrath to an " Ah, well!" followed by the com-
pressed lips which so often betray that wrath " to
be kept warm" is being nursed within the breast.

It was with curiously different feelings that
the mother and son awaited the time when

Honor's conduct, as revealed by Jack Winthrop, should be in solemn conclave sat in judgment on, and, as a matter of course, condemned. For that time—for the *auspicious* moment when John should have returned from that interminable walk, when his brother farmer, "drat him" (I am afraid that, Sunday though it was, the worthy old lady did indulge in a mild imprecation or two on the head of her unconscious visitor), should have taken his departure, and when they two should be sitting comfortably (?) over their tea, Mrs. Beacham longed with a feverish and impatient craving. It was so hard, so very hard upon her, that she was perforce obliged to keep this weighty discovery within the limits of her own breast. A secret, like a very young man's forbidden love affair, is worth nothing unless you can divulge it to the one friend who promises with such solemn vows to keep it closely (as closely, poor confiding one, as you have done yourself); and had the widow Thwaytes chanced to "drop in" that Sunday afternoon — a step which that scandal-lover would infallibly have taken could the remotest surmise of the delightful existing field for gossip have reached her ears — the delinquencies of the absent Honor would very soon have become public property at Switcham. Such luck, however, as a visit

from her congenial humble friend was not, on
that day at least, in store for the busy irate old
woman, who, strong in the strength of her Sabbath silk gown and great in her conscious dignity
of mistress regent at the Paddocks, sat prepared
to make—certainly not the *best* of her young
daughter-in-law's shortcomings.

"Well, John, what do you think of *this?*"
was her startling exordium when Hannah had left
the room, and John—poor John—had no escape,
and no longer even a reprieve from listening to
abuse—abuse, it was to be feared, only too well
merited—of his beloved one. "Well, John, this
looks nice, doesn't it? So milady stays in
Lunnon, not to nurse her father, as she'd have
us believe, but to go tearing about Hyde Park
with Mr. Vavasour! Pretty doings, upon my
word! I declare to goodness, if you take no
notice of *this*, I shall think you're just gone clean
out of your mind, and are only fit for an asylum,
so you are."

She stopped, more from lack of breath to proceed than from any immediate prospect that appeared of John's responding to her attack. He
felt called upon, however, to make some reply
to what sounded like an implied accusation of
lukewarmness, and of a disposition to "take
things" far more easily than he was in the

humour to do. His mother's abrupt onslaught
had, however, already produced an effect directly
contrary to what the indignant old lady had intended. She had either forgotten or ignored the
sensible proverb which saith " Scald not thy lips
in another man's porridge," and had aroused in
her son that fraction of masculine dignity which
causes its possessor to resist interference in the
management of his house and *harem*. Besides,
John's love for the beautiful object of Mrs.
Beacham's jealousy was still far too strong for
him to endure patiently the hearing his wife
found fault with by any other than himself; and
this being the case, his reply did not greatly tend
to Mrs. Beacham's satisfaction.

" Jack Winthrop is a chattering fool. I daresay he mistook Honor for someone else, for one
of young Vavasour's sisters probably ; and even
if she *was* riding in the Park, where's the mighty
harm ? It was but yesterday he saw her—*says*
he saw her, at least—and it's quite time enough
to pull her up if she says nothing of it herself
next time she writes, which will be to-morrow if
I'm not mistaken." And John, having so said,
pushed back his chair with the evident intention
of closing the conference. His mother, however,
was not to be thus cheated of her treat. She
had not been waiting for six mortal hours to

be put off with such a stupid shuffle as that!
No! For once in his life John should hear reason, let what would come of it, and if there was
no one else to tell him the truth, his mother
would do *her* duty, and point out to the in-
fatuated man what, in this crisis of his fate, was
his !

"John, John!" she said, lifting up a stub-
born finger warningly; "if I hadn't heerd and
seen this myself, I never could—and that's the
truth—have believed it. To think that you, a
man grown and with a man's blood in your veins,
should let a woman lead you by the nose like
this !"

"Nonsense, mother!" with an unsuccessful
effort to laugh the matter off. "No one is leading me, or thinking of leading me, by the nose,
as you call it. Honor is a silly girl, I don't
say she isn't, and she's fond of a horse; and if
her father—gad! how I hate to speak of the
fellow !—if her father put it into her foolish head
to ride, why ride she would, nor I don't blame her
neither. So, mother, let you and I hear the rights
of it before we blame her; and what's more—
you'll forgive my speaking"—approaching nearer,
and his breath coming shorter as he spoke—"but
if you would remember, mother dear, not to
speak to anyone in the village about this—story

—of Honor and the—the Park, I should esteem it very kind, and—"

"Oh, my dear, you may make yourself quite easy," snorted the old lady. "I'm not the bird to defile my own nest. It won't be through *me* if disgrace comes upon the family, and if *you* like to encourage your wife in her goings on with gentlemen—"

"Come, come, mother," broke in her son; "I must not have my wife spoken of, before she deserves it, as if she was a—a gay woman. I beg your pardon, but you make me more angry than I ought to be; and it isn't right, mother, God's book says it ain't. 'Blessed are the peacemakers,' we are told, and grievous words only stir up anger, they do; so let's keep from 'em while we can. I'm expecting to hear from Honor to-morrow, and if she says she's coming home and writes about this foolish ride of hers, why we shall be sorry then, poor pretty creature, that we said a word against her." And John, perfectly unconscious of the strangely mixed feelings, the half fear—a dread unadmitted even to his own breast—that Honor both deserved and would be visited with punishment, wished his mother "good-night," and left her to her reflections.

CHAPTER IV.

MRS. BEACHAM WRITES A LETTER.

THE late post on Monday (the eventful Monday it
was—for we have retrograded twenty-four hours
in our story in order to recount what happened
on that Sabbath afternoon at the Paddocks—the
eventful Monday it was which Honor spent with
Arthur Vavasour on horseback first, and afterwards in that feverishly enjoyable Richmond dinner), the second post, brought no letter from the
truant, and John's brow grew ominously dark as
he turned over his numerous business-like-looking
epistles, and amongst them found no dainty missive
in a fair running hand, and adorned with an en-
twined H. B. in mingled shades of brown and
blue, by way of monogram.

"There now! What did I tell you?" exclaimed
his mother triumphantly. "I was as sure as sure
could be, she wouldn't write. Guilty consciences
never do. And another time, my dear, I hope

you'll attend to your mother, old as she is, and act accordingly."

John made no reply to this aggravating little speech. Fortunately for him, the day was not one of rest, neither was the hour meal-time; so that the unhappy husband could escape from the irritating attacks of Mrs. Beacham's "deadly weapon." In truth, he was in no mood to listen patiently to the "I told you so," and the "You see, I was right," of the old lady's equivocal sympathy. His anger—hard to rouse in downright earnest against the beautiful girl, young enough, as the poor fellow often told himself, to be his daughter—had aroused at last to almost boiling-point; and, as is often the case with self-constrained but naturally passionate men, the change now lay in the probability that he would visit still more heavily than they deserved the indiscretions of the culprit, and that in his anger he would not even *remember* mercy.

Finding him still silent, Mrs. Beacham, accustomed from long habit to watch the changes on her son's countenance, glanced up at it from her eternal knitting, and was startled, strong-nerved woman though she was, at its stern rigidity, and at the colour—that of a livid leaden hue—which had taken place of the usual ruddy brownness of his cheeks.

"John, what *is* the matter? My gracious me, boy! you look as if you were going to faint."

The old woman had risen hastily from her chair, and, standing before him, had laid her two hands upon his arms, holding him thus, while with anxious motherly eyes she peered into the face of him who, being all the world to her, she loved with such a jealous and exacting devotion. For the first time in his life, John answered her shortly, and with what his mother, making scant allowance for the condition of his mind, chafed under as disrespect.

"Bother!" he said gruffly, putting her aside with one hand, while he donned his wideawake with the other. "I'm all right. What *should* be the matter?" And then, in a more collected voice, and with a more composed manner, he added, "I shall go to town to-morrow, mother, by the 10.30 train. I've no end of business to-day—other people's business, or I'd let it all go to Hanover, for what I cared. But for that, I wouldn't be so many hours before going up to see what that scoundrel Norcott is after with my wife; for, by Heaven"—and he struck a blow upon the old oak floor with his ash-stick that was enough to test the solidity of both—"by Heaven, I begin to think that there's more than we know of in his sending for her in the way he did. That

illness of his was all a sham—I'm pretty sure of
that by this time; and then his having Vavasour about her"—and John ground his strong
white teeth together as he said the hateful words—
"looks as if there was something devilish up with
the rascal. God knows! I've more than once had
a fancy—why, I couldn't tell you any more than
the dead—that all wasn't square about Rough Diamond. It was no business of mine to inquire into
it. If young Vavasour's been stuck, why, I shall
be sorry, that is, if—"

He stopped abruptly; for there were circumstances connected with the possible victim of Colonel
Norcott's rascality that would effectually check
any feelings of pity which John might be inclined
to entertain for him. Could the mother who bore
him have looked into the heart of her only child
that day, she would bitterly have repented the
stirring-up of the smouldering fire within which
her words—uttered, as so many dangerous words
are uttered, without much thought of future consequences—had effected. It is easy, terribly easy,
to raise the demon of suspicion and jealousy in
the human breast. Were the laying of the same
an equally facile task, or one equally congenial to
the unregenerate nature of men and women, there
would be fewer of the crimes consequent on the

strength of our worst passions to record, fewer
blighted lives, fewer consciences burdened with
the weight of scarcely bearable remorse. But
though the woman, whose tongue had wagged
(without ulterior design, but simply as a consequence of her own maternal jealousy) to such fell
purpose, could not read the heart she had unconsciously been working up to madness, she yet experienced something very like uneasiness when
John, with the heavy cloud still lowering over
his brow, and with the ruddy brown half-vanished
from his cheeks (so changed was he since the
poison of suspicion had suffused itself through his
veins), left her alone to ruminate on the past, and
anticipate darker doings in the future than she
had either hoped or calculated on. That John—
the dearly-beloved of her aged heart, the son of
whom she was so justly proud—could prove himself, under provocation, to be of a very violent and
passionate nature, she had not now to learn. He
had done his best to subdue and conquer his con-
stitutional sin; a sin, however, it was that might
and. did lie dormant, and indeed half forgotten,
within him, from the simple fact that it required
the great occasions that happily are comparatively
rare in all our lives to bring it into notice and
action. The blow struck in a moment of ungovern-
able rage at Frederick Norcott's unprotected head

had for a time, as we already know, filled John
Beacham's breast with remorse and self-reproach.
He had been very angry with himself, very angry
and ashamed; but that shame and anger had not, in
any degree, either softened his nature or disposed
him to any especial leniency towards his victim.
On the contrary, the soreness produced by self-
condemnation, and by imagined loss of caste, only
served to better prepare the mind of the man for
the reception of evil suspicions, and of perilously
active venom; and when John Beacham left the
quiet little parlour, and the tardily-repentant old
lady, who, when it was too late, would gladly have
recalled her words, he was in the mood of mind
that leads, at down-hill pace, to crime.

After his departure Mrs. Beacham picked up
the ball of gray worsted that she had in her agitation allowed to roll away upon the carpet, and
recommenced the task of turning the heel of
John's lambswool sock. Click, click went the
knitting-needles, and steadily jerked the bony
wrinkled hands that held the pins; but, contrary
to custom, the thoughts of the aged woman were
wandering far away from the work in hand—
away with the son whose fiery passions she had
helped to rouse—away with the thoughtless girl
whose " cunning ways " (Mrs. Beacham's vials of
wrath were filled to overflowing in readiness for

Honor's devoted head) and artful, "flirty goings
on were hurrying her poor John into his grave."

Suddenly a novel thought occurred to her,
and, laying down her knitting-needles, the dis-
tracted old lady, who was not "good at" doing
two things at a time, set herself to "think it out."
She would write—such was the idea with which
the mother of invention had inspired her—to
Honor herself! It was true that neither cali-
graphy nor the art of "composition" were among
the gifts which nature and education had bestowed upon the ever-busy mistress of Pear-tree
House, but for all that she would—so she then
and there decided—give "milady" a piece of her
mind that would bring back that "artful faggot"
—Mrs. Beacham was angry enough to apply *any*
names, however opprobrious, to her daughter-in-
law—in double quick time to her husband and her
duty.

When a woman—especially one of unrefined
mind—sits down under the influence of wrathful
passions to write a letter, the chances are greatly
in favour of her pen running away with her dis-
cretion—that is to say, of her using stronger
expressions, and of her doing a good deal more
mischief, than she had intended. The not-over-
well-concocted missive, which occupied the worthy
old lady who penned it during two good hours of

the afternoon, and was posted in time for the early morning delivery in Stanwick-street, proved, as the reader will hereafter learn, no poor exemplification of the truth of this not very novel remark. There are moods of mind in which the receipt of even a judiciously-penned letter irritates and offends the weak vessel that requires both tender and tactful handling. The missive of autocratic Mrs. Beacham was neither tender nor tactful, and pretty Honor's fate and conduct were terribly influenced for evil by what appeared at first sight to be one of the most every-day occurrences of every-day life.

CHAPTER V.

IT is unfortunate perhaps, and decidedly suggestive, but so it undoubtedly is, that beauty leads
the wisest amongst us terribly astray in our judgment both of character and motives. What observer, dispassionate or otherwise, who looked—
were such a privilege granted to him—at lovely
Honor's face and form, lying indolently, lazily if
you will, upon her narrow couch (the iron bedstead
in the Stanwick-street lodging), would have been
able to allow, without infinite regret and caution,
either that she was *wrong*, or the least in the
world deserving of punishment? A creamy com-
plexion, slightly tinged with the most delicate of
rose-colours; a tumbled mass of fairest brown
hair—"off the flax and *on* the golden," as Miss
Pratt would say; blue eyes, "languid with soft
dreams;" and full crimson lips, moist with the
morning dew of youth and health,—composed a
sum of attractions very decidedly calculated to

disarm criticism, and to modify the verdict of "Guilty" with the strongest recommendations to mercy. "Youth" and "previous good conduct" were pleas which might be safely urged as extenuating circumstances in the case of poor Honor Beacham's feminine sin of truth-suppressing; and as with her fair face slightly flushed, and her long brown eyelashes sparkling with indignant tears, she read, for the second time, a letter which Lydia (alias Polly), cross and out of breath with the labour of mounting the attic stairs, had just deposited on the bed, it was easy to perceive that the process · of retribution had already, in some sort, commenced.

That letter, as the reader will have no difficulty in guessing, was the one mentioned in the conclusion of the last chapter as the happy result of old Mrs. Beacham's interference with the connubial relations of her children. It took the well-meaning woman, as we already know, two hours in its concoction, and ran as follows:

"MY DEAR HONOR,—I write this to my great illconvenience, and to tell you that your conduct is not what it ought to be. John is not at home, but he was much surprised, as so was I to hear which we did by accident that you had been seen riding in Hyde Park in the place where I am told the ladies go, that honest women oughtnt to look at with a gentleman. I may as well say who Mr. Arthur Vavasour. Knowing the way you useter go on with that person I am not surprised at this, but John is, and I write to say that I cant have him vexed nor put out, and that you must come back directly and learn to behave yourself, and whats more, make yourself useful as you should do. Of course things wont be pleasant when you do come home, *that* isnter be expected, but we must take what Godamighty sends, and I knew when John married what it would be. I expect you will come back directly you get this, and I will send Simmons for you with the taxcart to meet the first afternoon train. John besides being so put about with what youve been doing is too busy with his horses to think of going himself."

A pleasant missive this to receive at early morning-time, when the recipient's head, a little turned by flattery and excitement, was full of fresh plans of pleasure, and was sedulously endeavouring to shut out intrusive thoughts of home, and to ignore the conscience-pricks against which it was so hard sometimes to kick! It would have been scarcely possible for the picture of what awaited her in her husband's dull *chez soi*, to have been brought with more unpleasant force before

the luxury-loving, indolent-natured girl, who was
becoming hourly more what is called *spoilt* by the
new life that she was leading. At no time greatly
drawn towards her mother-in-law (could it well,
all things considered, have been otherwise?), Honor,
at that inauspicious moment, almost loathed the
domineering, hectoring old autocrat, whose ways
were so very far from being *her* ways, and who
had thus unscrupulously laid bare to her the treatment that she, Honor, might expect when she
should return tardily, and, alas, not over-will-
ingly, to the sphere of the irritated old lady's
dominion. It may seem to some of my readers
that the thoughts and feelings, the likings and
dislikings of Honor, the married woman, bore but
scanty relation to those of the same individual who,
when a laughing, light-hearted, unselfish girl,
had found it so easy to win, not only golden opinions, but, still surer test of worth, the affections
of the small men and women committed to her
youthful guardianship. But while making this
objection, it is well to remind the critic of the
truth, that we none of us show what we really
are—either for evil or for good—till we are tried.
With youth, and beauty, and good spirits,—petted
too and much indulged, albeit she was " only a
governess,"—with the lamp of hope burning brightly before her, and with no shadow darkling over

the past, Honor *Blake* could have claimed small praise for being cheerful, yielding, and contented. It was in part, perhaps, owing to that very absence of trial that might be traced some of the striking changes that had apparently taken place in her disposition and character. Accustomed to be made much of, and dearly loving the *evidences* of being appreciated—well aware that her beauty was of that high and uncommon order which can be disputed by none, and that takes the senses, as it were, by storm—Honor, the stay-at-home wife of a staid and almost middle-aged man, had every chance of becoming discontented with the lot which at first sight, and before she had been allowed time to feel its flatness and monotony, had seemed to her all that was to be desired. That Mrs. Beacham — that the jealous mother-in-law, whom an angel from heaven would probably, under similar circumstances, have failed to please —should have had her lines also cast in the pleasant places of the Paddocks, had proved a real misfortune to Honor. " If she were *anywhere* but here!" had been often and often the girl's inward cry, when the peace of every moment, and the bright coming of each returning day, were disturbed and darkened by the small aggravations of John's crabbed and exacting mother. It is wonderful, the power that *one* person possesses to make or mar the comfort of a household. The constant *fears* of " something coming," the dread of words being taken amiss, the fretful answer, or even the mute reproach of shrugged-up shoulders, and a peevish sneer, can make to a sensitive nature the interior of a home that outwardly seems fair enough a daily, hourly purgatory. Poor Honor! As she lay upon her bed, thinking how very near the time had come when she must perforce exchange the delights, mingled though they were with the bitterness of self-reproach, of her present existence for the uncongenial company, the harsh sarcastic words, and the contemptuous looks of her unloving mother-in-law, her heart sank within her with disgust and fear.

" I cannot do it!" she said half aloud. "And John, too! What will he say to me?" And at the thought of her husband's displeasure, the wife who had lacked moral courage to speak the truth began to feel that, rather than face those two outraged and indignant spirits, she would gladly flee to the uttermost parts of the earth, and be at rest. To be alone—to work for her bread—to suffer hardship in every miserable and even degrading fashion—all this appeared to Honor (she being at the age and of the nature to jump at conclusions, and to imagine no evil equal to the present ones) infinitely, ay, a thousand thousand times, preferable to putting her pretty neck again under the yoke of angry Mrs. Beacham's thrall, and to the endurance, from morning's dawn to evening's light, of that unpleasant old lady's disagreeable form of being good and useful.

The idea of obeying her mother-in-law's behests, and returning with the least possible delay, did not, after the first shock of reading the letter, either form any portion of Honor's thoughts, or tend in any degree to increase her troubles. Go, till she had fulfilled one or two of her remaining engagements, she *would not*. To that conclusion she had come at *first*, and being one of those exceptional characters—characters, I suspect, more fanciful than real—whom a silken thread can lead, but who, like the Celtic animal that shall be nameless, turn restive when coercion is the order of the day, young Mrs. Beacham, resenting the old lady's tone of authority, set herself, with a determination of which one short year before she never would have believed herself capable, against that distasteful dose, the swallowing of which she knew (none better) to be her duty. Perhaps—we do not say it would have been so—but perhaps had *John* written to her, even angrily, this wrong-headed, but still warm-hearted, young woman might have been a trifle more amenable to reason, and better disposed to bear with patience the lot that she had drawn; but John, as we well know, did not write to his young wife at this momentous crisis of her life. He was busy. Epsom was at hand. Betting, sporting men were daily finding their way by express trains to the Paddocks, and all John's interest, time, attention were taken up, so Honor entirely and *half*-gladly believed, by other cares and pleasures than those connected with herself. " He does not trouble himself enough about me either to write or to mind whether I am here or there," she said with a sigh, as, standing before her small mirror, she noted self-complacently each of the undimmed beauties by which she believed her husband set so little store. " He does not care enough about me to be displeased if I ride with Arthur Vavasour. His mother says so—the tiresome old thing!—but I don't believe her; and she shall not—no, she *shall* not—have the satisfaction of thinking she has frightened me into obedience;" and with that doughty resolution Honor descended her many flights of stairs to breakfast with her newly-found and outwardly affectionate relations.

CHAPTER VI.

WHAT, SELL ROUGH DIAMOND!

THE breakfast meal at No. 13 Stanwick-street, not being either a varied or a luxurious one, did not occupy much of Colonel Fred Norcott's valuable time. It commenced, however, frequently at so late an hour, owing to the stay-out habits over night of the master of the house, that twelve o'clock often struck before the table was what Mrs. Norcott called "cleared," and the room ready for company.

Which company consisted usually, at the time of Honor's stay, but of one visitor—*the* visitor whom, for reasons best known to himself, Colonel Norcott was ever on the watch to conciliate and flatter. Arthur Vavasour's appearance in Stanwick-street was usually so timed that his host's horses—animals chiefly devoted at that period to the use of his daughter—should be walking up and down before the house in readiness for Mrs. Beacham's appearance. On the eventful Tuesday

morning—the Tuesday in Epsom holiday week—
which was hereafter to be a strongly marked one
in Honor Beacham's memory; Colonel Norcott,
departing somewhat from his accustomed habits,
was early astir—so early that at a little after
eleven he might have been seen, his cigar between his lips, standing on the steps of the house
he occupied, and evidently waiting for some
person whose coming was longer delayed than the
Colonel found altogether agreeable.   At last,
walking briskly round a corner, with a very preoccupied expression of countenance, and swinging
in the air a light riding-whip with the manner
of one lost in thought, Arthur Vavasour, the
individual expected by Honor's impatient parent,
appeared in sight.

"By George! you're late," Colonel Norcott
said, pulling out his watch and displaying it re-
proachfully before his friend. "I haven't more
than five minutes to spare.   Five?   I haven't got
three!   But if you've anything you want particularly to say to me, I—"

"You will wait—you *must* wait," Arthur
broke in imperiously.   "I tell you what, Colonel
Norcott, I can't stand the bother and the wear
and tear of this any longer; Rough Diamond,
as *we* know, is all right again, and the odds
are—"

"Five to four on the favourite! We all know that. What then?" and Fred replaced his cigar between his lips, and smoked away with a *nonchalance* which, to an excited man, was not a little provoking.

"What then? Why, simply this: I'd rather sell the horse, upon my soul I would, than go on in this way. If Rough Diamond loses—"

"Well, if he does?"

"Nonsense, man, what's the use of asking? you know nearly as much of my affairs as I do. You know how devilishly I'm dipped, and how everything depends on my horse winning the Derby to-morrow."

"Well, and he will win it. Don't be a fool. I mean don't be out of heart. I'm sure if I thought there were the ghost of a chance against him, I should be pretty considerably down in the mouth too. Why, man, I've backed the favourite with every farthing I'm worth, and—"

"Ah, yes—I know; but my case is different. Only fancy if old Dub was to find out (which he would be almost sure to do if the horse didn't win) that the brute is mine, and has been all along; what a row there would be! And then there's that infernal fellow Nathan—it's ruinous work renewing—so ruinous that, by Jove, I sometimes think—though of course I couldn't decide

anything without speaking to you. I sometimes
think whether it wouldn't be better—you see it
would never do for the old fellow to get wind of
these confounded bills—I sometimes think whether
it wouldn't be the best thing I could do to let
Lord Penshanger have Rough Diamond, and so
get out of the infernal bother of the business
altogether."

Fred Norcott, at these words turning a hot
and angry face to his companion, looked by no
means at his pleasantest. "What, sell the favourite!" he said. "By Jove, you must be mad !
I couldn't allow or hear of such a thing. I must
say that—but I beg your pardon, Vavasour; you
can understand that when a man has so much at
stake he loses his head, and hardly knows what
he's talking about. The fact is that Honor—that
poor girl in there" (and he pointed to the house,
before which they had been slowly pacing to and
fro) "is deuced miserable with that brute of a
farmer fellow that she married. She's staying on
with me because he and an old mother that he
has bully her so confoundedly between them; and
I should be glad to know if any tricks were to be
played on Rough Diamond (and I'll answer for
nothing if there's any change made) what would
become of that poor child? *I* shouldn't have a
home to offer her, and—but, by George, there are

the horses! Honor will be down in a minute,
and I shall be late," consulting his watch again,
" if I'm not off to Waterloo in double quick time.
Not going down to-day, eh? Well, there's no
accounting for tastes. See you at Opera to-night,
I suppose? And on receiving an affirmative nod
from Arthur, who already had his foot on the
first step of No. 14, Colonel Norcott went his way
towards the station, where almost countless crowds
were waiting to be conveyed to the same goal—
namely, the racecourse on Epsom Downs.

"What a lovely morning! I should like to
be out of doors the whole entire day!" exclaimed
Honor, as she and Arthur rode along the least
frequented road within the precincts of the Regent's Park, "and what is more, I long to be in
the country. Lydia had a holiday on Sunday, and
she says that all the beautiful chestnut-trees in
Bushy Park are in full blossom, and I *should* so like
to go there! Have you ever seen the avenue?
Mrs. Norcott has not, and she would like, she
says, to drive there this afternoon better than anything. Mr. Vavasour, couldn't we do it?" in a
pretty tone of beseechment. " I have so little more
time; and"—her checks flushing, half with anger
and half with shame at this betrayal of her home
secrets,—" I have had *such* a letter to-day! so
cross—so unfeeling! O, Mr. Vavasour, I am

afraid," looking very piteous, "that it will be all so dreadful when I go home. What *shall* I do? I almost wish that I had never come to London, the Paddocks will seem so dull, so miserable when I go back!"

"Miserable? Are you *quite* sure of that?" coming nearer, and resting his hand on the pommel of his companion's saddle. "Don't think me *very* selfish, but I should not like you to be too happy, Honor, not *too* happy when you are away from me. You sweet, beautiful creature!" gazing passionately on her downcast eyes, "why did not I see you, know you, in the lost time gone by, when you *might* have loved me, Honor? Am I too bold, too vain, to think, to hope that had we met sooner—met before you were tied and bound to another man—we two might have been happy? Speak to me, Honor. How can you be so cold, so quiet, when I—"

He stopped, half afraid, in that public spot, on the well-frequented road, where the girl's striking beauty attracted every passer's eye to gaze upon her lovely face, of the emotions which his words had so evidently aroused within her breast. At that moment, judging from outward signs—from the rapid rise and fall of the bosom, shapely as that of the glorious statue that entranced the world, and from the changing colour of her

rounded check—the accusation of coldness was not
altogether warranted by appearances. And yet
from those signs and symptoms the inference
which Arthur drew was very decidedly a wrong,
or rather an exaggerated, one. Honor was not
in the least what is called "in love" with the
man whose own passions and wild worship of
his neighbour's wife were making such desperate
work within his inner man. Almost utterly reckless had those days of constant communion with
her made him. He had cried havoc and let loose
the dogs of contending passions within his breast;
and if he had ever, when the waves of temptation were beginning to rise and swell, said unto
them with an honest and true heart, "So far shalt
thou go, and no farther," that time was long since
gone and over, and the submission of Cecil Vavasour's son to the great enemy of mankind was an
accomplished and a melancholy fact. But partly
perhaps because the man who really feels an over-
powering passion has less chance of *moving* the
object of that passion than has the hypocrite who
feigns a devotion which he is far from feeling,
Honor Beacham did not, as I said before, *love*
Arthur Vavasour. *Like* him she did; and greatly
did she prize his devotion, his delicate compli-
ments, his evident and irrepressible appreciation
of the attractions for which her busy unsophisti-

cated husband, the man whose affections were not
for the moment, but for Time, appeared to care so
strangely little. But although the eloquent blood
that rose to neck and brow had not its source in
the inner, and to Arthur the undiscovered, depths
of her affection, although the visible palpitations
of her heart could not with truth be traced to the
consciousness of harbouring one unholy or forbidden thought, still Arthur's words and sighs
and glances produced upon this child of nature
effects precisely analogous to those which might
have been displayed had the love which he pro-
fessed and felt been returned tenfold into his
bosom.

"I did not mean to be unkind and cold," she
stammered. " Quiet, Nellie !" (to the mare she
rode, and whose mild *caracoles* her own agitation
was provoking). " It was all my fault for talking
about going home ; and, Mr. Vavasour—"

" Call me Arthur," he broke in impetuously ;
" even you, who grudge me every word that is
not stiff and formal, even you can see no harm in
—when we are alone together—calling me by my
name ? Honor, I—"

She put up a warning finger, smiling as she
did so after a fashion that would have turned a
steadier head than Arthur Vavasour's. She did
not mean to be " coquettish ;" there was no pur-

pose in her heart to lure him into folly and madness. Honor's were very simple, but at the same time very cowardly, tactics — tactics, however, which have lost ere this more silly giddy women than even vanity itself. In *public* glad to please, and feeling, really feeling pity for the man whose passion she understood without reciprocating it, Honor would " smile, and smile, and smile," and seem to love; whilst in *private*—but then, to the best of her powers, and with an ingenuity of which none but a frightened woman could have been capable, she strove, and with good success, to postpone *sine die* the evil hour when she would perforce be brought to book, and when the lover whose *attentions* she would be more loth to lose than she the least suspected would insist on the decided answer which would render further trifling impossible—in private Honor might almost have been mistaken for a prude.

" How can you want me to call you Arthur," she said, with the bright smile that lit up her countenance like a sunbeam, " when you know it would be wrong—so wrong (and that is the best way to find out what *is* wrong) that you would, or I should, be always in a most dreadful fright lest I should forget myself, and say it when other people were present? O, how I *do* hate doing underhand things! I wish now, only it is days and days too late, that I had written everything I was about to the Paddocks. Then they might have abused me for being wilful and fond of London, and plays, and amusing things; but they could not have hated and despised me for being false."

"But," said Arthur with a caress in his voice, which Honor, novice though she was, was at no loss to feel and understand—"but there are so many things which pass, that one cannot say to everyone—many things which are not *wrong*, as you call it, but which people at a distance would not enter into, and had better therefore know nothing about. And so they have been worrying you with letters, you poor darling, have they? Wanting you to go back, and—"

"O, yes," Honor cried, brimming over with her wrongs, her yearning for kind sympathy, and with the self-pity which ever exaggerates the misfortunes which our precious *self* is called upon to endure—"O, yes, and Mrs. Beacham—she *is* so disagreeable; you don't know half how disagreeable she can be, orders me to come home, and threatens me with all sorts of horrid things. I am to be scolded and taught my duty, and," blushing beautifully, "someone has told *them* that I have been riding in the Park with you, and—Ah, Mr. Vavasour, I feel quite frightened, and I would rather

do anything in the world almost than go back
again to the Paddocks!"

"Anything?" he asked, throwing as much
meaning into the word as the human voice was
capable of expressing; but Honor, who was far
as the poles from comprehending the evil that was
in his thoughts, said eagerly,

"Indeed yes! anything! I would be a governess—you know I was a governess before—
I would go out to service—be a ' Lydia,' " and
she smiled a little bitterly, " if I could only never,
never see Mrs. Beacham's face again."

An expression which she took for amusement,
but which was in reality indicative of very unholy
triumph, passed over Arthur Vavasour's dark,
handsome face.

" Don't laugh at me," Honor said plaintively.
" You *can* have no idea how hard it is to live with
John's mother. Nothing I do is right, and—and,"
in a lower voice, " I know she sets him against
me. She has written to tell me that I must go
home to-day; but my father says I am to lay our
not going upon him, so here I shall stay! I know
I shall be in a dreadful scrape, and that it is only
a case of putting off, and—"

" But why *only* a case of putting off, as you
call it? My darling Honor—forgive me; the words
slipt out unawares—you know I would not offend

you willingly; but the best as well as the worst
men are liable to mistakes. Only tell me why
you, so young, so beautiful, so formed for the
enjoyment of everything that is bright and happy,
should be condemned to pass your days in such an
existence as the one you describe at the Paddocks?
It has always seemed to me," he went on, leaning
towards her, and looking with eyes of eager passion into her face—"it has always seemed to me
an act of the most miserable folly for people—married people—who do not *suit*, remaining together:
both would often be equally glad to part, to go
their respective ways, to live another and a more
congenial life; and yet from some foolish unreason-
ing scruple, from fear of what the world would
say, or from want of courage to take the first step,
they go on through all their lives, making each
other's existence a burden, 'when both might
separately have been as happy' as we are any of
us fated to be in this ill-managed world of ours,
where happiness is so rare a thing."

Honor glanced at him with rather a puzzled
look in her blue eyes. Strange as it may seem,
she did not even now comprehend his meaning.
That he was advising her to leave her home was
too plain to be mistaken, but that there was to be
sin—sin, that is to say, greater than that which she
could not but feel would be incurred by deserting

her husband and her duties—never occurred to this poor foolish child of nature. But although she did not comprehend, and could not fathom, the depths of her false friend's guilt, yet her womanly instinct led her to evade the responding to his suggestion. His last words also, and the tone of sadness in which they were spoken, riveted her attention, and, catching almost gladly at an excuse for changing the conversation, she said sympathisingly,

"What do you mean by ill-managed? Surely *you* can have no reason to think this world an unhappy one! If there exists one person in it who ought to be happy, it is you—you and your wife," she added, with a little sigh which again misled her companion into a blind and senseless belief in his own power over her affections. "You have everything, it seems to me, that human beings can hope for or desire—youth and health and riches, living where you like, and always seeing and enjoying the beautiful things that money can buy; and then going abroad, seeing foreign countries, and—and—"

"And what? Tell me some more of my privileges, my delights; make me contented, if you can, with my lot. At present it seems dark enough, God knows; and if—but I am a fool, and worse, to talk to you of these things; only, if I thought that you—you, who are an angel of purity and love and peace—would sometimes think of me with pity, why, it would give me courage, Honor, would make me feel that I have still something to live for, something to bind me to an existence which I have begun to loathe!"

Honor listened to this outpouring of real or fancied sorrows like one who is not sure whether she dreams or is awake.

"Mr. Vavasour!" she exclaimed, "what *can* you mean? At your age, with a young wife who loves you, and with" (blushing slightly) "the hope of the dear little child that will so soon be born, it seems so wonderful to hear you talk in this way! What is it?" warming with pity as she watched the young worn face prematurely marked with lines of care—"would you like to tell me?—I am very *safe*. I have no one" (sadly) "to confide in; and you have just said that my sympathy would be a comfort to you."

She laid her little ungloved hand — she had taken off her gauntlet to caress the arched neck of the pretty thoroughbred *screw* she rode—upon her companion's arm as she spoke, and so fully occupied was she with her object (namely, that of inducing Arthur to trust her with his sorrows), that she was scarcely conscious of the warmth with which he, pressing his hand upon the caressing fingers, mutely accepted the tribute of her sympathy.

"Ah, then," she said—the slight *soupçon* of a brogue, as was often the case when she was eager or excited, making itself apparent—"ah, then, you will remember I am your friend, and say what it is that lies so heavy on your heart?"

For a moment he looked at her doubtingly; and then, as though the words broke from him as in his own despite, he said in a low husky tone:

"What purpose would it answer, what good would it effect either for you or me, were you to learn that I am a villain?"

CHAPTER VII.

MEA CULPA.

A VILLAIN! Arthur Vavasour—the "fine," noble-hearted, brilliant gentleman to whom this simple-minded Honor had so looked up, and of the loss of whose friendship she had been so afraid that she had "led him on"—the silly woman knew she had—to fancy that she loved him better than she did her husband—was he in very truth a man to be avoided, shunned, and looked on with contempt? She could not, did not think it possible. He was accusing himself unjustly, working on her compassion, speaking without reflection : anything and everything she could believe possible rather than that her friend should deserve the odious epithet which had just, to her extreme surprise, smote upon her ears. Before, however, she could give words to that surprise, Arthur spoke again, and with an impetuosity which almost seemed to take away his breath poured forth his explanation of the text.

"Yes, a villain! You may well look astonished; and I expect, when you know all, that you will turn your back upon me, Honor, as all the world must; that is, if the world *has* to be taken into my confidence, which I still trust it will not be. There are extenuating circumstances though, as the juries say; and perhaps, if I had been better *raised*, I shouldn't have turned out such an out-and-out bad un as I have!"

He stopped for a moment to gulp down a sigh, and then proceeded thus:

"I think I told you once before how awfully I was in debt, and that it was the burden of debt that drove me into marrying poor little Sophy Duberly—the best girl in the world; but I *did not* love her (more shame for me), and whose affection, poor child, is so much more of a torment than a pleasure to me. Well, enough of that: the worst is to come; and if *you* can tell me, after hearing it, that I am *not* a villain, why, I am a luckier dog, that's all, than I think myself at present!"

Honor, feeling called upon to make some response, muttered at this crisis a few words which sounded like encouragement; but Arthur, too entirely engrossed with his *mea culpa* to heed this somewhat premature absolution, continued hurriedly to pour forth the history of his sin.

"You would never believe, you who are so young, so ignorant of the world's wickedness, what the temptations are which beset a man. Pshaw! I was a boy when I began life in London, and there were no bounds to my extravagance, no limits to what you in your unstained purity would call my guilt. I sometimes think that had my poor father lived, or even if I had possessed a dear mother whose heart would have been made sore by the knowledge of my offences, I *might* (God knows, however; perhaps I was bad in grain) have sinned less heavily, and have been this day unburdened by the weight of *shame* that oppresses me both by night and day. Darling Honor!—you sweet warm-hearted child! why were there no loving eyes like yours to fill with tears, in the days gone by, for me? In those days only guilty women loved, or seemed to love; and not a single good one prayed for or advised me. And so—God forgive me!—I went on from bad to worse! For *them*—for those worthless creatures whose names should not be even mentioned in your hearing—I expended, weak vain idiot that I was, thousands upon thousands, which, being under age, I raised from Jews at a rate so usurious that it could scarcely be believed how they could dare to ask, or any greenhorn be such a fool and gull as to accept, the terms. And

then, reckless and desperate, *afraid* to confide in
the mother who had never shown me a mother's
tenderness, I played—I betted on the turf—I—in
short, there is no madness, no insane extravagance,
of which, in my recklessness and almost despair, I
have not been guilty. But the worst is yet to
come. You remember that I bought Rough Diamond for a large sum of your husband. I gave
him a bill at six months' date, renewable, for the
amount; and John—he behaved as well as man
could do, I must say that—promised that it should
remain a secret that the colt was mine. Well,
some little time before my marriage—that marriage being a matter to me of absolute necessity—
old Duberly grew anxious and uneasy at my being
so much at the Paddocks. He had an idea, poor
dear old fellow, that I could only be there on account of matters connected in some way with
racing. So he wrote to my mother, of all people
in the world, for an explanation, and she naturally
enough referred him to me. Then, Honor, came
the moment of temptation. I *could not*—I positively could not, with my expectations, my almost
certainty, and John Beacham's too, of Rough Diamond's powers—part with him to any man living.
So—it was an atrocious thing to do; I felt it at
the moment, and Heaven knows I have not
changed my opinion since—I allowed Mr. Du-

berly—allowed! humbug!—I told him that the horse was not mine, and, liar that I was, that I had nothing to do with the turf!"

"It was very bad," murmured Honor; "but I suppose that if Mr. Duberly had thought the contrary, he might have refused his consent to your marriage, and then his daughter would have been wretched. Still, indeed, indeed, you had better—don't you think so now?—have been quite open with him. If you had said—"

"Yes, yes, I know; but who ever does the right thing at the right time? And, besides, I could not be sure, as you have just said, and knowing old Duberly as I do now, that he would have allowed his daughter to be my wife if he had been told the truth. His horror of what he calls gambling is stronger than anything you can conceive. I hear him say things sometimes which convince me that he would rather have given Sophy to a beggar—a professional one, I mean—than to me; and if he *had* acted as I feared, what, in the name of all that is horrible, was to become of me? The tradesmen, the name of whose 'little accounts, is legion, only showed me mercy, the cormorants! because of the rich marriage which they believed was to come off; while the Jews, the cent-per-cent fellows—but what do you know of bills and renewals, of the misery of feeling that a day of

reckoning is coming round—a horrible day when
you must either put the gold for which those devils
would sell their souls into their grasping hands,
or by a dash of your pen plunge deeper and deeper
into the gulf of ruin and despair? But there are
other and more oppressive debts even than these,
Honor—debts which I have no hopes of paying,
except through one blessed chance, one interposi-
tion of Providence or fate—for I don't suppose
that Providence troubles itself much with my
miserable concerns—in my behalf."

"And that chance?" put in Honor, imagining
that he waited to be questioned.

"That chance is the winning of the Derby to-
morrow by Rough Diamond. I have no bets, at
least nothing but trifling ones, on the race; but
if the horse wins, his value will, as of course you
know, rise immeasurably, and with the money I
can sell him for I shall be able, for a time, to set
myself tolerably straight. Your father—whose
horse you have, I suppose, hitherto fancied Rough
Diamond to be—has, he tells me, backed him for
all that he is worth. My reason for not doing so
has been that I am not up to making a book, and
that the debts of honour I already groan under are
sufficiently burdensome without incurring others
which I might not be able to pay."

"How anxious you must be and unhappy!"

Honor said pityingly. "But there is one thing which puzzles me, and that is, how you could keep all this a secret from your wife. Surely she would have been silent; surely she might have softened her father, and made all smooth between you."

"She might; but I could not risk it. Sophy is very delicate; and then there has been such entire confidence between her and her father, that it would have been almost impossible for her to keep anything from him. No; as I have brewed, so I must bake. I can only hope the best; and that, or the worst, will very soon be no longer matter for speculation. The devil of it is —I beg your pardon, I am always saying something inexcusable—but really the worst of it is, that the fact of my mother's intention of fighting my grandfather's will is no longer a mystery. Old Duberly's fortune is, as all the world believes, very large; but at the same time he is known to be what is called a 'character,' and that his eccentricities take the turn of an extraordinary mixture of penuriousness and liberality has been often the subject both of comment and reproach with people who have nothing to do but to talk over the proceedings of their neighbours. In short—for I am sure you must be dreadfully tired of hearing me talk about myself—the world, my

cursed creditors included, would be pretty well
justified in believing that my worthy father-in-
law would flatly refuse to pay a sum of something
very like fourteen thousand pounds for a fellow
whose extravagance and love of play were alone
accountable for the debt ; one, too, who has
nothing—no, not even a ' whistle'—to show of
all the things that he has paid so dear for.   Disgusting, is it not?   And now that you have
heard the story,—I warned you, remember, that
it was a vile one,—what comfort have you to bestow on me?   And can you, do you wonder at my
calling the world—my world, that is—a miserable
one? and is it surprising that, in spite of outward
prosperity, of apparent riches, and what you call
good gifts, I should sometimes almost wish to exchange my lot with that of the poorest of the poor,
provided that the man in whose shoes I stood had
never falsified his word, or lived as I have done
and do, with a skeleton in the cupboard, of which
another—one, too (forgive me, dear, for saying so),
whom I not greatly trust—keeps, and must ever
keep, the key?"

Honor paused for a moment ere she answered,
and then said, in a gentle and half-hesitating way
(they had turned their horses' heads some time
before, and had nearly arrived at Honor's temporary home), "I almost wish you had not told

me this; but we are neither of us very happy,
Mr. Vavasour, and must learn to pity one another. Perhaps—I don't know much about such
things—but perhaps I ought to say that you were
wrong; only, I am sure of this, that, tempted as
you were, *I* should have done no better. It must
have been so very difficult—so very, very fright-
ening! In your place I should never have had
courage enough to speak the truth; and I hope
—O, how I hope!—both for your sake and my
father's, that your horse may win! But am I to
say," she whispered, as with his arms clasped
round her slender waist he lifted her from the
saddle, "am I to say to him, to my father, that
I know about Rough Diamond? I should be so
sorry, from thoughtlessness, to repeat anything
you might wish unsaid."

He followed her into the narrow passage, where
for a single moment they were alone, and the craving within him to hold her to his heart was almost
beyond his power to conquer. Perhaps,—we owe
so much sometimes to simple adventitious circumstances,—but for the chance opening of a door on
the landing-place above, Honor would at last
have been awakened to the danger of treating
Arthur Vavasour as a friend. She was very sorry
for him; but she would have been more distressed
than gratified had he pressed her to his heart with

all the fervour of youthful passion, and implored her to trust herself entirely to his tender guardianship. On the contrary, seeing that he simply asked if Mrs. Norcott were at home, and reminded Honor of her wish to see the famous chestnut avenue, and of the practicability of realising her wishes, pretty Mrs. John Beacham tripped upstairs before him with a lightened heart, in search of the *chaperone* who was ever so good-naturedly ready to contribute to her pleasures.

CHAPTER VIII.

JOHN BEACHAM MAKES A DISCOVERY.

PEOPLE, especially imaginative ones, are apt to talk a good deal about coming shadows and presentiments of evil, becoming especially diffuse on the subject of the low spirits which they feel or fancy they have felt previous to any great and dire calamity. In my humble opinion such warnings lie entirely in the imagination, and, moreover, those who prate about this gift of second sight are apt to forget the million cases of *unannounced* misfortunes to be set against the isolated instances of anticipated evil. Amongst these million cases we may safely cite that of Honor Beacham on the afternoon of that famous Tuesday when, with complaisant Mrs. Norcott for her duenna, she strolled with Arthur Vavasour under the avenue of arching trees, then in their rich wealth of snowy beauty, which leads, as all the world well knows, to

" The structure of majestic frame
Which from the neighbouring Hampton takes its name."

Had Honor either been a few years older, less constitutionally light of heart, or more experienced in sorrow, she would never have been able so entirely—as was the case with this giddy young woman—to cast off the sense and memory of her woes. A reprieve after all is *but* a reprieve; and the consciousness that each moment, however blissful, serves only to bring us nearer to its termination, ought to and does fill the minds of the thoughtful with very sobering reflections. But, as I have just remarked, Honor's constitutionally happy spirits buoyed her up triumphantly on the waters whose under-swell betokened a coming tempest, and throughout the two swiftly-passing hours which she spent in the beautiful park with Arthur Vavasour by her side, she, recklessly setting memory and conscience at defiance, was far happier than she deserved to be.

The "pale and penitential moon" was rising over the Hyde-Park trees as the open carriage drove into Stanwick-street, and Honor, half pale and remorseful too now that the hour was drawing near when she must *think*, promised, in answer to Arthur's whispered entreaty, that no commands, no fatigue, no dangerous second thoughts, should cause her to absent herself that night from the theatre, where she was to enjoy one of their *last* pleasures, he reminded her, together. She ran upstairs—a little tired, flushed, eager, beautiful. Would there be — she had thought more than once of *that* as they drove homewards — would there be any letter for her upon the table in the little sitting-room where what Mrs. Norcott called a "heavy tea" was set out for their delectation? Would there—she had no time to speculate upon chances; for her quick eye soon detected a business-like-looking missive directed to herself, and lying on the table in front of her accustomed seat.

With a feeling of desperation—had she delayed to strive for courage the letter would probably, for that night at least, have remained unread—she tore it open and perused the following lines, written in her husband's bold, hard, rather trade-like writing, and signed by the name of John Beacham :   .

"DEAR HONOR,—I suppose you have some excuse to make for yourself, though *I* can see none any more than my mother does. You seem to be going on at a fine rate, and a rate, I can tell you, that won't suit me. I have been at the house you lodge at to tell you that I shall take you home with me to-morrow; so you had better be ready early in the day. My mother thinks you must have been very badly brought up to deceive us as you have done, and it will be the last time that I shall allow you to spend a day under your father's roof."

Poor Honor! Poor because, tottering, wavering between good and ill, it required but a small impetus, given either way, to decide her course. If it be true (and true indeed it is) that grievous *spoken* words are wont to stir up anger, still more certain is it that angry sentences written in moments of fierce resentment, and read in a spirit of rebellion and hurt pride, are apt to produce direful consequences. When Honor, with the charm of Arthur Vavasour's incense of adulation still bewildering her brain, and with the distaste which the memory of old Mrs. Beacham's society inspired her with strong upon her, read her husband's terse and unstudied as well as not particularly refined epistle, the effect produced by its perusal was disastrous indeed. Dashing the passionate tears from her eyes, and with a wrench throwing off the dainty little bonnet and the airy mantle in which Arthur Vavasour had told her she was so exquisitely "got up," she prepared herself to meet again at the New Adelphi the man whose influence over her, aided by the unfortunate circumstances in which she was placed, had more than *begun* to be dan-

gerous. On that night, her *last* night—but—and
here Honor laid down the brush with which she
was smoothing out her rich rippling tresses—
but must it be indeed, she asked herself, the
last night that she would be free? The last
night that she might hope to pass away from
the wretched thraldom, the detested daily, hourly
worry of her unloved and unloving mother-in-
law? Must she indeed return (and at the un-
spoken question her heart beat wildly, half with
terror and half with the joyful flutter of anticipated freedom), must she obey the *order*—for order
it was, and sternly, harshly given—to place herself once more in Mrs. Beacham's power, in the
home which that domineering and unkind old
woman had rendered hateful to her?

To do Honor only justice, there was no glim-
mering, or rather, to use a more appropriate
word, no overshadowing, of guilt (of guilt, that is
to say, as regarded the straying of the thoughts to
forbidden pleasures) in her desire—a desire that
was slowly forming itself into an intention—of
making a home for herself elsewhere than at the
Paddocks. She had arrived, with the unreflecting
rapidity of impulsive youth, at the decision that
John had ceased to love, and was incapable of
appreciating either her beauty or her intellect.
His mother, too—and in this decision Honor was

not greatly in the wrong—wished her anywhere rather than in the house where *she* had been accustomed to reign supreme; and this being the case, and seeing also that poor Honor could expect (for did not those two threatening letters proclaim the fact?) nothing but unkindness on her return, there remained for her only the alternative—so at least she almost brought herself to believe—of separating herself from those with whom she lived in such continued and very real unhappiness.

During all the time that was employed in tastefully arranging the hair whose rich luxuriance scarcely needed the foreign aid of ornament, and in donning the dress fashioned after the *décolletée* taste of the day, but which Mrs. Norcott— who entertained an unfortunate fancy, common to bony women, of displaying her shoulders for the public benefit—assured her was the *de rigueur costume* for the theatre,—during all the time that Honor was occupied in making herself ready for the evening's dissipation, the idea of " living alone" haunted and, while it cheered, oppressed her. Of decided and fixed plans she had none; and whether she would depart on the morrow, leaving no trace to follow of her whereabouts, or whether she would delay her purpose till a few days should have elapsed after her enforced return

to Pear-tree House, were subordinate arrangements which this misguided young woman told
herself that she would postpone for after consideration.   For the moment, the prospect of listening
to the most exciting of dramas, and of seeing (for
she was easily pleased) the well-dressed audience
of a popular theatre, bore their full share in
causing the future, as it hung before Honor's
sight, to be confused and misty.   The convenient
season for thought was to be *after* this last of her
much-prized pleasures ; and when this bouquet of
the ephemeral delights by which her senses had
been so enthralled would be a memory and a
vision of the past, the young wife told herself that
the time for serious reflection should begin.

An hour later, in a box on the pit tier, listening with every pulse (for Honor was too new and
fresh not to take an almost painful interest in
the half-tragic and perfectly-acted play) beating
responsive to newly-aroused sensations, the young
wife of the Sandyshire farmer attracted a good
deal more attention and admiration than she—
entirely engrossed with the scene and the per-
formance—could, vain daughter of Eve though
she was, have supposed to be possible.   Her dress,
made of inexpensive materials, but of pure, fresh
white, and unadorned, except with a bunch of
pale-blue convolvulus, matching another of the

same flower in the side of her small, fair head, was a triumph of unpretending simplicity. Alas, however, for the fashions of these our days! For well would it have been—before one pair of eyes, gazing on Honor's attractions from the pit, had rested on her beauty—could some more efficient covering than the turquoise cross, suspended from her rounded throat by a black velvet ribbon, have veiled her loveliness from glance profane! Honor little knew—could she have had the faintest surmise that so it was, her dismay would have been great indeed—Honor little knew whose eyes those were that for a short ten minutes—no more—were riveted, with feelings of surprise and horror which for the moment almost made his breast a hell, upon the box in which she was seated. John Beacham—for the individual thus roused to very natural indignation was no other than that much-aggrieved husband—had learned from chattering Lydia, on his visit to Stanwick-street, that Mrs. Beacham was on that evening to betake herself to the New Adelphi with—the name went through honest John's heart like a knife—Mr. Vavasour and Mrs. Norcott. They were gone—"*them three*," Miss Lydia said—to "''Ampton Court" for the afternoon; but the Colonel—he was expected back before the others. Perhaps the gentleman—the parlour-maid was totally ignorant of

the visitor's right to be interested in Mrs. John
Beacham's movements—perhaps the gentleman
would wait, or it might be more convenient to
him to call again when the Colonel would have
come back from the races. She didn't believe that
Colonel Norcott would go to the theatre. She'd
heard some talk of his going to the club; but
if—

John, who had heard with dilated and angry
ears the main points of these disclosures, and who
was very far from desiring to come in contact
with the man whom upon earth he most despised
and disliked, waited to hear no more, but, striding
hastily away, surrendered himself, not only to the
gloomiest, but to the most bitter and revengeful
thoughts. That this man—unsuspicious though
he was by nature, and wonderfully ignorant of the
wicked ways of a most wicked world—should at
last be roused to a sense of the terrible possibility
that he was being deceived and wronged was, I
think, under the circumstances, only natural ; and
in proportion to the man's previous security—in
proportion to his entire trust, and complete defi-
ciency of previous susceptibility regarding Honor's
possible shortcomings—was the amount of almost
uncontrolable wrath that burned within his aching
breast. For as he left that door, as he walked
swiftly down the street, and remembered how he

had loved—ay, worshipped—in his simple, inex-
pressive way, the lovely creature who was no
longer, he feared, worthy either of his respect or
tenderness, no judgment seemed too heavy, no
punishment too condign for her who had so outraged his feelings and set at naught his authority.
Full of these angry feelings, and boiling over with
a desire to redress his wrongs, John Beacham
repaired to the tavern where he was in the habit,
when chance or business kept him late in London,
of satisfying the cravings of hunger. Alone, at
the small table on which was served to him his
frugal meal of beefsteak and ale, John brooded
over his misfortunes, cursing in bitterness of spirit
the hour when he first saw Honor Blake's bewildering face, and exaggerating—as the moments
sped by, and his blood grew warmed with one or
two unaccustomed "tumblers"—the offences of
which she had been guilty.

He was roused from this unpleasant pondering
by the clock that ticked above the tall mantelshelf
of the coffee-room sounding forth the hour of eight.
Eight o'clock, and John, who never passed a night
if he could help it in London, had not yet made
up his mind where to spend the hours which must
intervene before his morning meeting with his wife.
Enter the doors of Colonel Norcott's abode—save
for the purpose of carrying away the headstrong,

deceitful girl whom he, John's enemy, had so
meanly entrapped—the injured husband mentally
vowed should be no act of his: not again would
he trust his own powers of self-command by finding himself, if he knew it, face to face with the
object of his hatred.   From the hour, and to that
effect he registered a vow—from the hour when
he should regain possession of his wife, all communication of every kind whatsoever should cease
between Honor and the bold bad man in whose
very notice there was contamination and disgrace.
From henceforward Honor, so he told himself,
would find a very different, and a far less yielding,
husband than the fool who had shut his eyes to
what his mother's had so plainly seen.   Henceforward the young fop and spendthrift, whom for the
boy's father's sake he had encouraged to visit at his
house, should find it less easy to make an idiot of
him.   Henceforward—but at this point in his cogi-
tation a sudden idea occurred to him; it was one
that would in all probability have struck him long
before, and would certainly have shortened the modest repast over which he had been lingering, if
he had entertained—which certainly was not yet the
case—any doubts and suspicions of a really grave
character relative to Arthur Vavasour's intimacy
with his wife.   That she had deceived him with any
design more unpardonable than that of temporarily

amusing herself was a thought that had not hitherto
found a resting-place within the bosom of this
unworld-taught husband; though that Honor had
so deceived him was a blow that had fallen very
heavily upon him. Thoroughly truthful in his own
nature, and incapable of trickery, he had been so
startled and engrossed by the discovery in Honor's
mental idiosyncrasy of directly opposite qualities,
that for a while he was incapable of receiving any
other and still more painful impression concerning
her. To some men—especially to those unfortu-
nately-constituted ones who see in " trifles light as
air" "consummation strong" of their own jealous
fantasies—it may seem strange that John Beacham
should not have sooner taken the alarm, and vowed
hot vengeance against the destroyer of his peace.
That he had not done so was probably owing to a
happy peculiarity in his constitution. He was a
man too well aware of his own hasty temperament
to rush without reflection into situations to which
I can give no better or more expressive name than
that of *scenes*. To quarrel with, also, or to offend
the son of Cecil Vavasour would have been a
source of infinite pain to the man whose respect
and affection for his dead landlord would end but
with his life ; his wish, therefore, that Arthur had
been and was no more to Honor than the companion, in all innocence, of her girlish follies, was.

the father to the conjecture as well as to the belief that so it was.

Probably, had John been returning for business purposes that day to the Paddocks, the idea which did then and there occur to him, of hurrying off to the New Adelphi, in order to *judge for himself*—as if in such a case any man could judge justly!—of Honor's conduct and proceedings, would never have entered his head. It was a sore temptation only to look again, sooner than he had expected, at his wife's beautiful face; and as, in memory as well as in anticipation, he dwelt upon it, the strong man's heart softened towards the weak child-like creature whom he had sworn to honour as well as to love, and it would have required but one smile from her lips, one pressure of her tender arms, to persuade him once again that *she* was perfect, and that if fault or folly there had been, the error lay in himself alone.

Perhaps in all that crowded house—amongst that forest of faces that filled the boxes and gallery to the roof—there was not one, save that honest countryman, whose attention was not fixed and absorbed that night on one of the most sensational melodramas that have ever drawn tears from weak human eyes. At another time and under other circumstances John Beachman, who, strong-bodied and iron-nerved man though he was, could never

keep from what he called making a fool of himself
at a dismal play, would not have seen unmoved
the wondrous tragic acting of one of the very best
(alas, that we must speak of him in the past!) of
our comic actors: but John Beacham, on the night
in question, was not in the mood to listen with interest to the divinest display of eloquence that ever
burst from human lips. He was there for another
and less exalted purpose: there as a spy upon the
actions of another—there to feast his eyes (for,
as I said before, in spite of all her errors, his heart
was very soft towards the one woman whom he
loved) on the wife who had defied his authority,
and, possibly, made him an object of ridicule.

He had not been long in the unconspicuous
place he had chosen before, not far removed from
him—in a box, as I before said, on the pit tier—
he descried his unsuspecting wife. Such a start as
he gave when first he saw her! Such a start that,
had not his neighbours on the next seat been fully
occupied with the Stage, they must have perceived
and wondered at his agitation. At first he could
hardly bring himself to believe—so changed was
she, and so wondrously beautified—that it could
in reality be his own Honor whom he saw there,
radiant in her glorious loveliness, and with that
loveliness—ah, poor, poor John Beacham!—displayed, in a manner which almost took away his

breath, to the gaze of hundreds upon hundreds of admiring eyes.

Until that moment—the moment when he saw her the admired of all beholders, in the evening toilet which so enhanced her attractions, it may be doubted whether John had ever entirely realised the exceeding beauty of the wife whom he had chosen. In her simple morning-dress, and especially in the little coquettish hat which he had sometimes seen her wear, the honest farmer was quite willing to allow that Honor was prettier by far than nine out of ten of the pretty girls that tread the paths of life; but it was in the dress, or rather undress, that evening dissipation rendered (according to Mrs. Norcott's dictum) necessary that young Mrs. Beacham became—in her husband's eyes—not only a marvel and miracle of loveliness, but a source of such exceeding pain to that inexperienced rustic that in his agony of jealous susceptibility he clenched his muscular hands together till the blood well-nigh burst from his finger-ends with the strong though all involuntary compression of his fingers.

For there was more than the sight of those white shoulders to rouse the demon of anger in his breast; there was more than the memory of the woman's deceit to harden his heart against her; for beside, or rather behind her, leaning over

those same white shoulders in most lover-like and
devoted fashion, stood Arthur Vavasour, the man
of whom his mother had in her rude fashion warned
him, the man whose father had been not only his
(John Beacham's) friend, but his benefactor!

Whispering in her ear, calling the crimson
blush to her fair cheek—the husband saw it all!
And ah, how at that moment poor John hated that
dark handsome face—the face of one looking so
like a tempter sent to try the faith and virtue of
an angel only too ready, so it seemed, to fall!

Will any of my readers—any, that is to say,
who have in their own persons borne the burden
and the heat of human passions—marvel that this
man, spurred by the spectacle before him—the
spectacle not of *fictitious* crimes and sorrows, for
there was a side-scene in which a deeper melo-
drama was being enacted for his benefit—should
have "lost his head" under the pressure of such
unwonted excitement?

Something—it was not common sense or reason, for he was long past any safeguard they
could render him — *something* retained the man,
whose passions were so rapidly growing to be his
master, in the place which, between two elderly
playgoers who were entirely absorbed by the
" scene," had been assigned to him — retained
him, that is to say, till such time as, the act being

over, he could move from his place without causing public excitement and commotion.

When the curtain fell, and the rushing, rustling
sound betokened that the spectators, over-wrought
and excited, were stretching their limbs and re-
freshing their brains by a change of scene and
posture, John Beacham, following a sudden and
uncontrollable impulse, and with no fixed purpose
within his brain or choice of words upon his lips,
staggered like a drunken man to the box where
Honor, breathless with eagerness and her fair face
flushed with excitement, had just—in entire and
happy ignorance of her husband's proximity—
turned her glossy head to talk over the startling
incidents of the play with Arthur Vavasour.

CHAPTER IX.

JOHN PROVES HIS RIGHT.

As he opened the box-door, a ray of reason—there is often on such occasions something sobering in the mere presence of strangers—threw a composing light over John Beacham's troubled brain. He was not, as we already know, a man who loved excitement and "went in" for sensation; on the contrary, his country habits and his rather matter-of-fact nature unfitted him for taking part in any emotional scene, of what kind soever it might be.

Entering the box, he took off his hat with in-stinctive politeness; but that duty performed, he laid his hand—it was as we know an honest one, but heavy enough withal—on Honor's snowy shoul-der. What followed was the work almost of mo-ments; but rapid though it was, the scene remained engraved on Honor's memory for ever. As the iron fingers pressed into the delicate flesh — he could not guess, poor man, that her *first* feeling when he entered had been one of gladness—she uttered a sharp cry of pain, and cast an appealing glance—for John's wild looks and violent action frightened her—at Arthur.

Was it in mortal man, or rather was it in the man who loved her, and who almost believed his love returned, to remain neuter, absolutely neuter, in such a case as this? It was true, quite true, that the husband was *dans son droit*, and had a right to resent as an insult the interference in his wife's behalf of any man that lived. Of this important truth, however, Arthur remembered nothing. Blinded by passion, disturbed at a moment when, forgetful of all the world beside, he was distilling what he believed to be successful poison into the ear of the woman he adored, this spoilt child of sin, who had never denied himself a pleasure, or made during his whole stormy manhood a single sacrifice either to others or to duty, resented the entrance of Honor's unconventional husband into his private box, as if that husband were in fact the encroacher, and *he* the lawful possessor of the prize.

White, ay, almost livid with rage, he wrenched away the hand that held the woman whom he delighted to protect, and would have spoken words of violence suited to the intemperate action, had not John Beacham, subdued for the moment by the sight of passions even stronger than his own,

commanded him in a tone of startling energy to
be silent.

"For your father's sake, young man," he said,
laying his broad hand for an instant on Arthur's
thin white lips — "for your dead father's sake,
make no ugly scandal here. If I believed you
worse than foolish, I would kill you as you stand
there! but I do not believe such evil of your
father's son. Go, sir, to your young wife; go
and repent you of your sins; and when we meet
again, God grant that I may have a better opinion
than I hold now of the boy that Cecil Vavasour
loved in his life so well!"

Startled, overcome, and terribly confused, Arthur stood as if transfixed; while John, after
hastily wrapping the trembling Honor in her
opera-cloak, led her, without another word spoken,
from the box.

In perfect silence—a silence only broken by
the woman's violent trembling as she hung helplessly on her husband's arm—the re-united pair
left the crowded theatre together. Honor moved
along as if mechanically, dreading the moment
when she would be alone with the man of whose
violence she had just experienced such unpleasant
proof, and feeling already, with terrible force, the
bitter contrast between her lot as it had lately
been, and her fate as it loomed darkly, wearily

before her. *Resigned* she did not feel. The contrast was too great, too sudden ; and, to speak the truth, the aspect of John in his rough overcoat, his driving-gloves, and country-made hat, did not exactly tend either to put Honor in good humour with her husband, or to reconcile her to the loss of half her evening's amusement.

Had there been in the woman's conscience the load of even the smallest secret guilt, *fear* would have usurped the place of anger, and all idea of rebellion would have banished from her mind. But Honor's fit of trembling arose from no such hidden cause. No "sin," even of thought, hitherto "unwhipt of justice," caused her cheek to pale and her limbs to quake with fear. She was simply overwrought, over-excited ; and more than all, she was indignant. A woman—a beautiful one, that is to say—does not always calmly submit, even from a husband, to rudeness, when she has been accustomed to adulation ; or to coercion, when she has been placed upon a throne, and learned to think herself a "queen for life."

She was the first to speak—the woman usually is in embarrassing cases such as that I am describing. The man, who is as a rule less nervous and excitable, and who generally speaking has his senses more under his own command, is apt to hold his tongue, and rather dread the

breaking of the ice—the prelude to the startling
and unpleasant plunge from which he greatly
doubts that any good can possibly result.

"O, John!" Honor said, "where *are* you
taking me to? You might have waited till to-
morrow, and—and—I see you are so angry." And
bursting into tears, she leant her shapely little head
against the side of the cab in which John had
placed himself and her, and sobbed with almost
hysterical violence.

"Angry? I should think so," was his reply,
as he endeavoured to harden his heart against the
wilful girl whom yet (he was terribly ashamed of
the uxorious weakness) he ardently longed to take
to his heart and whisper the fond assurance that
she was forgiven. "I should think I *was* angry—
ay, and precious angry too. Why, now, I should
like to know how you came to act underhand
in the way you have done, and that, too, from
first to last? Why didn't you write that you
were riding about and amusing yourself? Why
did you allow us—my mother and I—to think
that your father was in difficulties, while all the
time he could afford to keep horses, and give you
all sorts of amusements? By George!"—and he
gave a blow on the floor of the cab with his stout
stick which must have sorely tested the strength
of both—"by George! if anyone—if the best

friends I have on earth—if the mother that bore
me had said a month ago that she had seen what
I have seen this night, I would not have believed
her; and now—"

"And now," interrupted Honor, her tears
checked as if by magic, and turning her large
indignant eyes full upon her husband, "and *now*,
what, pray, have you seen? You talk to me as
if I had done something wicked, something disgraceful; whereas the worst crime of which I can
excuse myself is a dread, a *horror*—I had better
say the truth at last—of living with, and being
tormented by, your mother. It is more than I
can bear to live with her. I would rather beg
my bread, rather be a servant a hundred thousand
times, than go back to Mrs. Beacham and be
treated as she has treated me. But," suddenly
letting down the window of the cab, and looking
out into the street, "you are not really taking
me back to Updown? John," clasping her hands
in wild entreaty, "I implore you not to let me
live again at Pear-tree House. I don't know why
it is—I can't account for it—but besides my being
frightened at your mother, I have a fear upon me,
a great dread, of that old house. Something, I
am certain of it, as certain of it as that I am pray-
ing to you for kindness now, will happen if you
take me home to Updown. I—"

"You are a goose, my dear, and don't know when you are well off. There, there, don't cry any more. We are close upon the station now, and people will think I have been beating you."

The cab drew up to the entrance of the South-Western terminus as he spoke, and Honor, feeling that remonstrance was useless, allowed her arm to be passed through that of her legitimate guardian, and herself to be seated, with a very unwilling mind, in the carriage that was to convey her, luggageless and nervous, to the country home which she had learnt to loathe.

CHAPTER X.

THE great day of the sporting year, the " maddest," if not exactly the " merriest " day, was close at hand ; and the world, both high and low, rich and poor, one *against* another, were on the *qui-vive* of excitement and the very tip-toe of expectation. Among these variously interested beings, one of those who had in reality most at stake, was Arthur Vavasour. Fortune, honour, credit, all were involved, and that to no limited extent, in the winning of the Derby race by that big-boned, coarse - made, but wonderfully *staying* horse, Rough Diamond. Time was (before the master passion had laid hold of, grappled with, and finally taken possession of this impulsive and ill-trained young man) when the result of the morrow's racing would have occupied his every thought, and would have seemed to his eyes the most important of all earthly considerations. And all-important indeed it was ; for spurred on

thereto by money difficulties, and being but of a
weak and unstable character, Arthur Vavasour
had, as the reader must have already gathered,
deceived, and to a certain degree outwitted, the
shrewd and rather obstinate old man, whose ideas
of honour and morality were so widely different
from his own. By marrying Sophy Duberly he
had for a time escaped the consequences of his
own reckless extravagance, and of the gaming
propensities, the knowledge of which would, as he
well knew, have entirely prevented the union between himself and one of the richest heiresses of
the day; but happiness had not followed upon his
sin, nor had a sense of security been the consequence of his deception.

That Mr. Duberly was not wholly without his
misgivings on the score of the young aristocrat on
whom his daughter's maiden affections were fixed
was evidenced by the fact that " nothing was
left," as the saying is, in Arthur's " power." The
allowance that " old Dub " made to his future
heiress was liberal to profuseness; and Arthur
himself, had he desired such an indulgence, might
have had his path paved with gold, provided always that he, the retired Manchester man, was
perfectly *au courant* of how the money was disposed of, and that his dearly-beloved Sophy trod
the same brilliant way, side by side and lovingly

with the partner of her life. More than this,
however, for his son-in-law at least, old Dub
was never likely to do. To have his penny-
worth for his penny, to keep his accounts regu-
larly and systematically, were, in his opinion,
among the first duties of man; and any *known*
neglect of these duties by his daughter's husband
would have annoyed and disquieted him. Well
aware of this "absurdity," as he considered it,
on the part of his father-in-law, Arthur had for
some short time after his marriage gone through
certain minor forms calculated to convey the impression that he was a "business man." A room,
called by courtesy his study, had been devoted to
his use; and a book dignified by the title of an
"account-book" was disfigured by certain scrawl-
ing entries in Arthur's large illegible hand, and
was supposed to contain a record of Mr. Vavasour's daily expenditure. Happily for him, old
Duberly had hitherto either taken his business talents for granted, or, like many other good-natured,
as well as slightly indolent people, had shrunk from
discoveries which might only tend to his own dis-
comfort, and the possible unhappiness of his child.
Sophy—the darling of his age, and the sunshine
of his luxurious home—was blithe and joyous as a
bird which has just found its mate; and this being
so, why was he to disturb her from her security,

and fill her unsuspecting mind with doubts and
fears which never might be realised? As long as
Sophy, who was a very *girl* still in simplicity and
buoyant spirits, went singing about the house (a
little heavy in step now, poor thing, for she was
very near to her hour of pain and travail), old
Duberly was well content to let everything remain
as it was, and to hope the best regarding his
young and outwardly very likeable son-in-law.
That there was any *great* harm in one who seemed
so frank, and who was too young as well as too
well-born (the Manchester man thought a great
deal of birth) to have had either much opportunity
or much temptation to sin, Mr. Duberly never for
a moment suspected; but in spite of this trust,
and gladly as he would have entirely confided in
his daughter's husband, there lingered, almost
unknown to himself, a grain—the very shadow of
a shade it was—of doubt; a doubt born of the
former visits of Arthur Vavasour to the Paddocks,
where lived the most beautiful woman that Mr.
Duberly had ever seen, and where the " tempting "
yearlings put on strength and muscle for the
arduous work that lay before them. That such
a doubt did linger in the old man's mind was a
fact of which he himself was almost ignorant.
Had any human being ventured to hint a syllable
in disparagement of Arthur Vavasour the blood of

the quondam cotton lord would have been up at
once, and he would have indignantly repelled the
insinuations of the enemy.   According to his own
belief he had placed implicit faith in Arthur's assurances that the turf and he were strangers, and
that his " occasional " visits to Pear-tree House
were either purely business ones, or were the natural consequences of his dead father's respect and
liking for honest, straightforward John Beacham.

It was the certainty that his father-in-law
had so believed, and in consequence of that belief
had consented to the already arranged marriage,
which was the main cause of Arthur's anxiety
that Rough Diamond should, by winning the
Derby, diminish the chance — a very slender
one he hoped and trusted—of Andrew Duberly's
discovering the trick—for trick it was—that had
been played upon him.   " Manchester man "
though he was, and somewhat rough in manner—
to say nothing of his living out of the pale of
Arthur's " world"—that young man nevertheless,
such is the force of moral worth, dreaded, more
than he would have cared to own, the betrayal to
his wife's father of the secret which, for all his
seeming carelessness, had not lain altogether
lightly on his bosom.   His debts—barring those of
honour, considerable though they were—troubled
him but little.   Tradesmen, however careful of

their own interests, will never press inconveniently for payment when they know for a certainty that in the family of their debtor there are assets sufficient to defray ten thousandfold the "little account" which added interest is yearly swelling. It was the floating paper, his debts to so-called friends, and above all, as I have just said, it was the guarding of his disgraceful secret, which, even under other circumstances than the present, would, on the day before the Derby, have made Arthur Vavasour's brow a clouded one by day, and broken his natural sleep by night. And even now—madly, passionately as he loved the woman of whom it was guilt even to think, and from whom, to his intense annoyance, he had been so suddenly and violently separated—Arthur could not avoid the frequent recurrence of the oppressive thoughts connected with his own falsehood, and the morrow's all-important event. Even on his way home on foot from the theatre—walking, contrary to his custom, because he desired time for thought previous to his return to home and Sophy—even then, with the memory of Honor's bewildering beauty still fresh within his brain, reflections born of his complicated troubles forced themselves upon his unwilling mind. What would happen to him if the favourite—a chance quite, of course, upon the cards—were distanced?

What would happen to him if—and the idea was not by any means a novel one—he could not trust the unprincipled associate in his scheme? what would happen if Honor's father should in some way or other—Arthur had never gone the lengths of guessing *how*—play him at the eleventh hour false?

These and sundry other such-like questions were easy enough — as tormenting questions usually are—to ask, but the responses to them were not in the present case forthcoming. Plodding on, with anything but a young man's elastic spring, Arthur wended his way to Hyde-park-gardens; and grievous as the truth must seem, there was not, in the certainty that one warm woman's heart would throb with joy at his return, a drop of balm to soothe the wounds from which he suffered. And reason good was there that so it should be, for those wounds were of his own inflicting—dealt by his own guilty hand, and not to be healed save by the slow and painful process of repentance and atonement. Slowly, then, and with a troubled spirit, this man, who to the world's eye appeared one of the most favoured of Fortune's adopted darlings, proceeded on his way. Arrived at the grand spacious house, with its marble portico, its solid pillars, and its sculptured ornamentation, which he called his home, he paused for a moment, looking up with some feeling of undefined surprise at the more than usual amount of light which found its way through the closed shutters of the several windows. Almost before, however, he had time to lay his hand on the bell, the door was softly opened by a servant who had evidently been on the watch for his arrival, and a low voice—the voice of the hall-porter, softened and subdued in compliment to the momentous occasion—informed the young master of the house that Mrs. Vavasour had half an hour before given birth to a fine boy, and was "as well as could" reasonably "be expected."

CHAPTER XI.

ON the whole it was a relief to Arthur that *les convenances*, according to old Dub's view of the matter, stood in the way of his being an eye-witness of Rough Diamond's capabilities on the Derby-day. His first feeling on hearing that Sophy's trial was over, and that he had a paternal interest in the small pink-faced fraction of humanity which the nurse introduced to him as his son, had been one of unmixed satisfaction. As he silently kissed the pale but wondrously contented face of the young mother lying so still and motionless on the pillow, Arthur's heart was full for the moment of the purest happiness that it had ever known; but the past—the inexorable and ever-pursuing past—treading on the heels of the present, embittered his transient joy, and destroyed, or at least darkened, all his prospects for the future. Almost before he had left the bedside of his trusting and silently rejoicing wife, the thought of the evil which a few short hours might bring about struck through him with an icy chill, while conscience with her probing pricks told him that he was unworthy of life's choicest blessings. For even then—even at the instant when his mind and heart should have been wholly occupied with the fair young mother of his child—a vision of his Irish love—of Honor's sweet caressing smile, and the exquisitely-moulded shoulders that had been, but one short hour before, so dangerously near to his caressing hand—rose up before him, and caused the bonds which united both him and her to objects unbeloved to be hateful in his sight. On the following morning old Mr. Duberly, in radiant spirits, and rejoicing over his grandson with a delight which struck Arthur as almost puerile in its character, gave his son-in-law plainly to understand that his place, for that day at least, was one within call of his marital duties. To watch by Sophy, to be ready if she should perchance express a wish to press his hand, or gaze lovingly on his face, were privileges which the affectionate old man would have found it hard to believe that Arthur might prize less highly than he did himself. The circumstance of that especial Wednesday being the Derby-day escaped his recollection altogether. Being himself totally uninterested in sporting matters, the idea that

Arthur would by any possibility place the result of the great race side by side as an affair of note with the all-important event of the previous day, namely, the birth of his son and heir, would have struck "old Dub" as simply ridiculous, and he was therefore quite prepared for Arthur's ready acquiescence in his views. The real truth was, as we already know, that Vavasour's interests were far indeed from being centred on Epsom Downs. To gain *the* race by means of his own good horse, Rough Diamond, was certainly to him an affair of vital importance; but, unaware of the fact that Honor had been taken from Colonel Norcott's house, and was already safe under her husband's protection, the desire to see her once again, by stealth or otherwise, was stronger than any other feeling, and to remain in the neighbourhood of the woman he adored was the dearest wish of his unregenerate heart.

Meanwhile, what was the reality regarding Honor Beacham's whereabouts, what her feelings, and how had her husband's sudden exertion of marital power affected her conduct?

The night-train by which she and John travelled homewards was due about midnight at Leigh, at which town it stopped for a few hurried minutes only, and then proceeded at express speed on its course south-westward. Happily for

Honor, they were not *tête-à-tête* in their compart-
ment.   Childlike, she caught at any delay, any
postponement of the explanation which was the
inevitable consequence of her folly and—in some
sort—her falsehood.   To keep back the truth—
not to tell that " whole," when on that " whole"
depends the *spirit* of the facts left half undisclosed
and to be guessed at—is, disguise it, mystify ourselves with what sophistry we may, *to lie unto our
neighbour*, and to deceive the one who trusts us.
It was the consciousness that she had so lied and
deceived, together with a certain amount of un-
investigated self-reproach as regarded the delight
which Arthur Vavasour's society had afforded her,
that caused Honor to shrink with nervous trepidation not only from her husband's question-
ings, but from the very sight of the keen-witted
and sharp-tongued old woman who already, as
Honor had every reason to believe, looked on her
with no favourable eyes.   Under these circumstances, the presence in the carriage which they
occupied of a sleepy old gentleman and a wideawake young girl, who was in all probability his
daughter, was a relief not only to Honor but to
John ; for he too, with all an honest, strong-
nerved Englishman's dislike to tears and domestic
tragedies, recoiled from the duty of saying harsh
words to the young wife, whose worst offence he

felt inclined to believe had been a love of hitherto undreamt-of gaieties, the consequence of which very natural tastes was the sin—one of omission rather than commission—of giving a false colouring to the state of affairs in Stanwick-street.

Already, so kindly was the man's nature, and so strong was his dislike to being what he called "ill friends" with those about him,—already had his displeasure begun to subside, and already had he begun to accuse himself of harshness in thus summarily dealing out hard measures against his wife. As she sat there silently by his side, the outline of her perfect profile just visible under the scarlet hood of her opera-cloak, and her pale lips quivering with the effort to conceal her emotion and check the tears that from moment to moment were on the point of escaping from their " briny bed," it would have required but little to persuade the strong man near her that in his dealings with that frail but fairest flower he had been little better than a brute.

They were within a mile or two only of Leigh before the silence that reigned between them was broken, and then it was John's clear and rather loud voice that awoke the elderly sleeper, and startled Honor from a very perplexing and wretched train of thought.

" Twelve o'clock, all but two minutes," Mr.

Beacham said, replacing a solid silver watch in his waistcoat-pocket. "We shall be at Leigh directly, and if there doesn't happen to be a fly there," he added, addressing himself more particularly to his wife, "we shall have to put up at the Dragon. The old lady expects *me*, and Simmons will be there, of course, with the trap; but you'd catch your death o' cold without wraps, and—"

"O, I don't mind! What *does* it signify?" Honor said impatiently, and even, as it seemed to John, a trifle crossly; whereas the hasty-sounding words were simply the result of the broken reverie, the seriousness of which made the question of a covering more or less upon her shoulders appear in the light of a very trivial affair indeed. Before, however, he could make any rejoinder to her impetuously-spoken reply the speed began to slacken, and a loud deafening "whistle" proclaimed the fact that their journey's end was reached, and that unless something like a miracle were wrought in her favour, a very short period of time must in the common course of things elapse before poor Honor would find herself once more in the dreaded presence of her exacting and unloving mother-in-law.

"Now, then, my dear," John said *kindly*, as Honor thought and hoped, when he returned to the train after a rapid investigation of the waiting

carriages ; " now, then, come along ! look sharp ;
there is a fly—the one from the Dragon—so
bundle in.   It wouldn't have done," he went on,
after they were seated, and the windows closed to
shut out the night air, " to have kept mother up
while I sent for this old rattletrap from the inn.
Mother's put out enough as it is, and I don't
know—upon my soul, I don't—how she'll take
our coming in upon her like this.   I tell you what
it is, Honor, my dear, you must try—indeed
you must—to pull better with the old lady.   I
thought you would at first ; but somehow everything seems to have gone wrong ; and then this
business—this staying in London—and—"

He stopped abruptly at this crisis in his dis-
course,—stopped because, his momentary passion
being over, the old feeling of inferiority to his
wife, the undefinable consciousness of her refine-
ment, her delicacy, her " good blood," her *lady-
hood*, as opposed to his roughness and plebeian
birth, gained ground again, and checked the
well-deserved reproaches that were hovering on
his lips.   Had Honor been at that moment clad
in her customary dress of neatly-made linsey, had
there been no blue flowers in her rippling hair, and
had there been no " jewelled cross" glittering on
her " snow-white breast," John would have been
twice the man he was—twice the man, that is, in

his power to speak out to his young giddy wife the truth which it was good for her to know. But this simple-minded rustic felt, as we all of us more or less have probably done, the influence of show, of adornment, of superior dress, above all of a soft, gentle *retenue* of manner which puts to shame and utterly condemns the violence of the more impulsive and the outspoken. Angry, justly angry as he had so lately felt with Honor, John's courage failed him when he commenced to reason with her on her shortcomings, and he paused, not knowing how to pursue a subject which could not fail to be displeasing to the youthful beauty whom he had so lately seen the admired of all beholders in the London playhouse. John little guessed — well would it have been for all parties had it been otherwise—what a very coward was at that moment the woman who, all unconsciously to herself, was making a poltroon of him. Trembling, shivering inwardly at the thought of the dreaded interview with her stern and relentless judge, Honor would have given much at that moment to have been certain of a friend and ally in her husband. It was her ignorance on this point, and not, as John suspected, the increased " fine-ladyism" which, unknown to herself, was evident in her air and tone, that kept her silent, even from mild words of apology and self-justification.

Ashamed, frightened, and thoroughly detesting the companionship to which her husband was about to condemn her, it was little to be wondered at that John Beacham, believing her to have taken refuge in a "fit of the sulks," relapsed into a silence which lasted till the wheels of the lumbering, misnamed vehicle, after grating for a few seconds along the well-known gravel, came to a stand before the ivy-covered porch of Pear-tree House.

If Hannah had seen that often-talked-of object of her awe and curiosity, an actual ghost, she could hardly have been frightened into a more violent start than that which jerked her stoutly-built person at the sight of her young mistress.

"My good gracious me! Who ever would have thought it?" she exclaimed, as she followed Honor's lagging footsteps into the little parlour. "Why missus never expected you, mum, not for a moment—and everything going on so quiet! Dear, dear! it was only this very day as missus was a saying—"

"O, I don't want to know, Hannah," said Honor wearily, as she threw herself on a sofa, a degree harder (if possible) and more comfortless than the one appertaining to the first-floor front in deeply-regretted Stanwick-street. "Please not to tell me what Mrs. Beacham said. And make

me a cup of tea, will you? I am very tired, and
I shiver so!"

She shuddered as she spoke, but that she did
so was more from inward cold than from the
effects of the outer atmosphere. There was certainly something terribly chilling to this young
and impressionable creature in the dingy, half-
lighted room, with its dusky curtains, its faded
carpet, and, above all, the work-a-day table co-
vered, as was its wont, with evidences of the old
lady's unflagging industry—with piles of house-
linen, placed there in readiness for the morrow's
inspection, for darning, marking, or the like; and
with batches of John's strong gray socks—articles
of toilet far more useful than ornamental. On
these uninteresting evidences of an active as well
as a frugal mind a solitary tallow-candle shed its
feeble light; and Honor, from whose vivid imagination the picture of the brilliant theatre with its
dazzling footlights and bright array of mere-
tricious beauty had not altogether faded away,
gazed around with feelings nearly akin to loathing
and disgust.

A momentary gaze almost it was, for before
she had time *quite* to realise the melancholy truth
that she was at home, John had settled accounts
with the Leigh charioteer, and was once more
by her side, and speaking in subdued tones to

Hannah, who, after the manner of her kind, was bustling about, and making as much noise in the doing so as possible.

"Don't make more row than you can help, there's a good woman," John whispered anxiously; "there's no use in waking up the missus. Bring a cup of tea, hot and strong, as quick as you can, and then take yourself off to bed."

Hannah made no reply to this exhortation, save by throwing a knowing glance at Honor, which that bewildered young person did not even attempt to comprehend. The mystery, however, did not take long to solve, for ere another minute had elapsed there was the sound of a creaking step upon the stairs, and Mrs. Beacham's chronic cough (a cough which the doctors said she would never lose but in her grave) heralded the approach of Honor's enemy.

Instinctively the young wife, as the gaunt figure of the old woman, clad in the sternest of nightcaps and the most uncompromising of flannel gowns, made its appearance in the doorway, turned an appealing face to her husband, thus mutely claiming his protection and support. Unfortunately, however, for this weak vessel, whose conscience was assisting to render her a coward, the language of *looks* was an unknown one to single-eyed John Beacham. In addition also to this ignorance, it would have been hard to make him understand that it was against his own mother that Honor, in that piteous glance of hers, entreated that he would array himself. He was experiencing at that moment one of the effects of a long habit of filial obedience and respect, and that effect was a real regret that his aged parent should have her rest disturbed, and her mind harassed by his wife's—to say the least of it—thoughtless conduct. John's affection for his mother was too deeply rooted to be easily shaken; and though he had, for a passing moment, been softened, quelled, subdued by his tenderness for his wife—though he had for a short while forgotten that Honor had, in more ways than one, braved, disobeyed, and utterly deceived him—yet, with the presence of the respectable and unimpeachably virtuous woman who had first opened his unwilling eyes to the culprit's errors, the remembrance of those errors crowded once more thick and fast upon him; so thick and fast that his very face grew darker and more serious, whilst Mrs. Beacham, happily unconscious that her appearance was not precisely a dignified one, advanced slowly, candle in hand, into the room.

CHAPTER XII.

MRS. BEACHAM REFUSES TO FORGET.

"Well, mother," John said airily, and with the laudable desire of making things pass off with ease and comfort to all parties—"well, mother, we've got Honor back again, you see; but I'm sorry you got up. I tried to keep Hannah quiet, but she's got a foot like a cart-horse, and a voice like a peacock, hang her!"

"I wasn't asleep, my dear," sighed the old lady, seating herself with a dignified air—the effect of which was slightly neutralised by the above-named dressing-gown and cap—"I wasn't asleep; it ain't easy to be with all that is going on;" and she folded her aged hands before her with an air of patient resignation, which was not without its effect upon poor John. For that excellent man, at this crisis of his hitherto unexciting life, was really very greatly to be pitied. Longing, above all things, for peace and quietness

—loving his young wife with a deep and passionate fondness, and sincerely wishing that his respected parent might find a dutiful daughter in his precious Honor — it was to him a terrible thought that a "scene" of some kind must inevitably take place before matters could run smoothly again between his womankind.

"Mother," he said desperately, "let bygones be bygones. Honor has been foolish enough, I know, and she had better not have made things out different from what they were; but there's no manner of use hammering on about what's past and over. So, Honor—there's a good girl—just tell mother you're sorry for what's happened, and let us all be friends again. It's the best way, to my thinking, times and over."

He laid his hand very lightly on his wife's bare shoulder as he spoke, giving the slightest of impulses to his touch; but, to his dismay, Honor, instead of obeying that impulse, recoiled from the pressure of his hand, and said in a low tone, but resolutely:

"I have done no harm. I am sorry, of course, if she is angry; but, John, you do not know—if you did, you would understand it all better—what your mother wrote to me. I would do anything for you—I would, indeed," she added passionately; "but *she* hates me—she always did; and

I will not—no, I *will* not humble myself before her!"

"You *will* not? There's for you!" cried the indignant old woman, roused to fury by Honor's resistance to her husband's wishes. "Didn't I tell you how it would be? Didn't I say that you had got rather more than you could manage in milady there? Why, only to look at her is enough, and more than enough for me. If *you* call *that*"—and she pointed with a fierce trembling finger at Honor's polished shoulders—"if you call *that* the dress of a modest woman, why you are a bigger fool, John, than I took you for. I should have liked to see *my* husband's face if *I* had made such a wanton of myself as to—"

"Come, come, mother, enough said," interposed John. "I don't like the way that young women get themselves up nowadays a bit better than you do; but she's in the fashion—Honor is, and anyway I won't have her called hard names even by you.—Honey, my dear," he went on more gently, as he noticed his wife's quivering lip, "you mustn't be so foolish as to think what you said just now. Mother doesn't hate you; she couldn't be so wicked, letting alone that you're not one that the worst woman—which God knows she isn't—could dislike. So, now *do*, for Heaven's sake, let us have done with it all. You're looking

as pale and as cold"—wrapping the opera-cloak
round her carefully, in order to conceal the smooth
white shoulders which were so obnoxious in his
mother's sight—" as cold as death, my dear.
Here, take a cup of tea; and, mother, suppose
you have a drop of something warm?—Here, Hannah, bring in the ' matarials'—as Joe Connor calls
'em—and let's make ourselves comfortable."

His voice—it was a very pleasant one at all
times—sounded loud and cheerful through the ill-
lighted room—it was a voice that his old mother
dearly loved to hear; but, just then, so uncongenial were her own feelings, and so hardened
was her heart against the girl whom she *really* believed to be " gay and giddy," if not worse, that
she refused to be softened by her son's cordial
tones.

" You may do as you please," she said, rising
in what was intended for a stately manner from
her chair, " but *I* shall not remain in the same
room with Mrs. John. Hate her, indeed! I never
heard such words. ' He that hateth his brother is
a murderer!'—and nobody before ever evened me
to that. I wish you good-night, John; and I hope
that God will give you both better thoughts. I
may forgive—but it isn't likely I should forget."

The door closed behind the jealous wrong-
headed old woman; and John, preparing me-

chanically to mix his nightly jorum of weak brandy - and - water, heaved a more weary sigh than had often escaped his lips.   There was something touching in the sound—proceeding as it did from one so habitually (at least to outward semblance) cheerful and *insouciant*—and Honor, hearing it, suddenly felt penitent and sympathetic.

"I am so sorry," she said softly.   "I know I was wrong—and, John, I should be so much happier if your mother would be kind to me.   It was more that—I mean more because of her—that I seemed to care to stay away—I—"

"There, there, my dear," he said, his arm round her waist, and drawing her towards him tenderly, "don't bother yourself any more about it.   We must all try to bear and forbear; and mother is old now—and old people have their fancies.   You, poor little thing," gazing pityingly on the wet eyelashes that swept her pallid cheeks, "I would make you happy, God knows, if I could. You are such a child still—and somehow, it seems to me that you were not made for this rough life of ours;" and John, loosening the hand that pressed the slender waist, sighed again even more discontentedly than before.

CHAPTER XIII.

ARTHUR CHEERS UP.

THE news that John Beacham had carried his wife
into the country, without even allowing that ill-
used young woman to return to Stanwick-street,
was communicated on the following morning by
Colonel Norcott to his young friend, to whom he
wrote a hurried note as follows :

"Only fancy ! John Beacham, after behaving
like a bear, carried off my poor girl, just as she
was, to Updown. I had half a mind to interfere ;
but the Derby before everything ! We shall meet
on the course, I suppose. If not, at the club afterwards. Good luck to Rough Diamond, and to us !
We are in the same boat. Sink or swim ?—with
me, at least.

"Yours in haste,

"F. N."

Many hours sped by after the receipt by
Arthur of this note ere the important telegram

arrived which told the world remaining in London
which horse had won "the race." In spite of
his mad love for Honor Beacham, Arthur Vavasour heard the news with all-absorbing rapture.
There were "take-offs," it is true, from his joy.
He was deprived of the pleasure of openly revelling
in the fact that a horse of his had won the Derby
by a head. Rough Diamond, running in the
name of Colonel Norcott, was generally supposed
to be the *bona-fide* property of that fortunate individual; but although he could not hold his head
high as the owner of a Derby winner, Arthur
could, and did, rejoice with exceeding joy over the
result of the race. He was, virtually, free from
the debts of honour which had so long oppressed
and disgraced him. The sale of the winner to the
highest bidder would enable him to walk once
more with a free step, and boldly, amongst the
young men his fellows. That the heir-apparent
of so fine a property as Gillingham Chace should
have been reduced to such shifts, and have suffered from such pecuniary anxieties as had sometimes rendered sleepless the luxurious couch of
Arthur Vavasour, may seem to some an ab-
normal, if not, indeed, an impossible, state of
things; but it must be remembered, in the first
place, that the heir to many thousands per annum
had been but for a short period legally "of age;"

and in the next, that the raising of money by that
individual would have been at all times—in consequence of Lady Millicent's well-known intention
to dispute her father's will—an affair very difficult
of arrangement.   Ever since his purchase of John
Beacham's powerful and, as his former owner—
one of the best judges in England—boldly af-
firmed, most promising colt, Arthur had seen,
with the confident eye of youth, a limit to the
annoyance which had so long pressed upon his
spirits. They had been very good-natured to him,
those sporting friends of his to whom he owed
some fifty, some a hundred, and *one* more hundreds than it was pleasant to remember. They
had bided their time.   Arthur Vavasour had been
such a mere lad when he became their debtor, and
the men were, without an exception, far older, both
in years and experience, than Lady Millicent's
thoughtless son; so, as I said, they had treated
the young man tenderly.   No cold shoulders had
been turned to him either at the clubs or on
the racecourse; and Arthur, thankful for the indulgence, was doubly glad of the opportunity
which his success afforded him of paying with
grateful thanks those who, somewhat singular to
say, had not ceased to be his friends.

Five minutes had scarcely elapsed after Arthur
read the welcome telegram, when he betook him-

self to the gratifying business of preparing for his
long-delayed settling-day. His first act was to
put himself in indirect communication with the
sporting earl who, as all the world was well aware,
possessed a purse long enough to gratify his lord-
ship's desire to become possessor of the Derby
winner; and his next object of interest was the
promised visit of Colonel Norcott, who, although
he did not greatly admire his character, had, both
as the nominal owner of Rough Diamond and the
father of Honor Beacham, peculiar claims on his
time and attention. Very early on that day, and
soon after receiving Fred Norcott's billet, he had
despatched a note to that gentleman's abode, and
in that note he had informed his friend of the interesting domestic reason of his absence on the
previous day from Tattenham Corner on that all-
important occasion.

"I will call in Stanwick-street about nine P.M.,"
so wrote the newly-made father, "when I hope to
find you at home, and shall be truly glad if there
is good news for us in the interim." Arthur was
well pleased to escape a meeting at "the club," *id
est, his* club, with Colonel Norcott. That gentleman
was in the habit—a propensity which was rather
annoying to Arthur Vavasour—of showing off, at
the Travellers', his intimacy with the popular young
heir of Gillingham, the former being well aware

that he stood on unsafe ground, and that it behoved him to make the most of such respectable acquaintances as fate, or rather conduct, had left him. The indomitable Fred, not content with linking his arm within that of Arthur Vavasour, when the two chanced to meet in the haunts of fashionable men and women, would, whenever he could either seize or make an opportunity for so doing, parade his acquaintanceship with his young friend in the most unwarrantable manner. It was in order to prevent a repetition of this inconvenience that Arthur Vavasour (who would probably have been more careful of hurting the Colonel's vanity had Honor Beacham still remained under his protection) indited the epistle above alluded to, namely, that which appointed Stanwick-street as a place of rendezvous between himself and the owner of his most cherished secret. Well aware of the fact that Colonel Norcott, who belonged to no regular "club," but only to a sporting *réunion* of doubtful respectability, was in the habit of making the best of his lodging-house dinner at home, Arthur Vavasour entertained but little doubt of finding his middle-aged friend (whose health, albeit he would have strenuously denied the fact, was beginning to betray some of the consequences of an ill-spent life) resting from the excitement of the day in the bosom, so-called by courtesy, of his family.

Sophy—the happy, grateful Sophy—watched over by loving eyes, and surrounded by all the comforts and luxuries that wealth could procure, was "going on," as the hall-porter was now officially instructed to say, "as well as could possibly be expected." Old Duberly, whose heart, in spite of the strength of his prejudices, had in it some very soft and tender spots, had as yet only partially recovered from the state of almost frantic ecstasy into which the birth of his grandson and the certainty of his daughter's safety had thrown him. It is true that he no longer insisted upon shaking hands (each time that he encountered them on the stairs or in the passages) with Arthur, the doctor, or maybe the nurse—anyone and everyone, in short, who could by any possibility sympathise with his grand-paternal joy. He was less demonstrative, and more quietly thankful to the God of all mercies for the great blessing that He had bestowed upon him; but for all that he was more outwardly composed; the old man's inward condition— whether sleeping or waking, alone or in company with his fellow-rejoicer by Sophy's bedside —was one of exceeding gratitude and bliss.

"I am thinking of going out for an hour, sir," Arthur said, suppressing with some difficulty one of the troublesome and desperate yawns

which a lengthened dialogue with his respected
father-in-law was apt to induce. "Sophy is
asleep, the nurse says, and I want to stretch my
legs and have a smoke."

Mr. Duberly, who as a rule was rather an
enemy to the favourite vice of the day, and who
had sometimes felt a little jealous when he had
seen his "girl's" white fingers busy in Arthur's
tobacco-jar, and pressing down with her dainty
thumb the *weed* into her husband's meerschaum,
was at that especial moment in too good a humour
not only with Arthur, but with the world in
general, for any idea of opposition to enter his
brain.

"Want a smoke, do you, eh?" he said good-
humouredly. "I don't know what you young
fellows are made of to stand drawing so much
poison into your lungs. And what you'll all be
like when you come to be my age is more than
I can guess. But get along with you, boy—
only don't be long, for Sophy may wake up
and want to say 'good-night.' *I* shall be in the
boudore though, ready, if anything's wanted."
And so saying, the doating old man, gathering
up his spectacles, and the newspaper which he
was in the habit of digesting with his dinner,
a meal which at that moment sat—if the truth
must be told — rather heavily on his stomach,

toddled out of the room, to pass a dozy hour or two within hearing of his daughter's gentle voice.

Meanwhile Arthur — his heart, despite of pretty Honor's absence, lighter than it had been for months—wended his way with the brisk step which is so sure a sign of youth and good spirits to not-far-distant Stanwick-street. As he approached the house he experienced a slight feeling of depression at the thought that it no longer contained the lovely woman by whom he fondly believed that his passion was more than beginning to be reciprocated. It was a melancholy fact, too, that as matters at present stood between him and John Beacham, there seemed little hope of resuming those *friendly* relations with the Paddocks which had been so fraught with happiness to himself, and, as he hoped, to the wife of his trusting friend. To the chapter of accidents only could Arthur—with the sanguine expectations of youth (of youth especially when backed by good looks and a winning tongue)—look, with any well-grounded hope, that his luck would in this instance befriend him, and point the way for further attempts to—what? Why to *ruin*, soul and body, the still innocent creature, the possession of whose beauty would soon be to him a worthless toy, and who, but for his selfish pursuit, might still be a valued wife and a happy woman in the sphere in which Providence had placed her.

As Arthur Vavasour stood on the doorstep of the house which only a few short hours before contained the being who possessed the terrible power of inducing within him the forgetfulness of his most sacred duties, keen regret for her loss was within his breast a stronger sensation than the satisfaction with his present lot, as regarded the relief from his dishonouring obligations which, in some natures, *might* have superseded all other and less commonplace considerations.

"He will know nothing more about *her*," was the thought that most occupied Arthur Vavasour when the door opened, and Lydia, more off-hand even and coquettishly dressed than usual, stood before him with the handle in her hand, barring, as it almost seemed—though *that* could hardly be, so intimate was Arthur in that unaspiring lodging-house—his further passage to the Colonel's presence.

"There's a note for you, sir," the parlour-maid said, in answer to Arthur's look of surprised inquiry; "they've gone out of town, both of 'em, and the Colonel said I was to give you the letter when you comed. I'll run and fetch it if you'll be so good as wait." And so saying

Lydia skipped away down the "back stairs" leading to the regions below; while Arthur, with a vague sense of uneasiness creeping slowly over him, silently, but not over patiently, awaited her return.

CHAPTER XIV.

ARTHUR FINDS HIMSELF DONE.

THE letter produced, after five minutes' delay, by the faithful Lydia, ran as follows:

" MY DEAR VAVASOUR,—You will be surprised to find that I have *absquattulated.* Beggars mustn't be choosers, and I should have been only too glad if circumstances had allowed of my remaining in England; but the fact is, I made a bad business of my book—hedged, and that kind of thing; so, having no chance left but to sell Rough Diamond, I did it on the nail. My beastly creditors have made London too hot to hold me, and as debts are transferable in these days, and be hanged to them! I must keep dark for the present, or they'll have me in *quod* in some confounded foreign place or other. Of course you are an exception; and when I am settled anywhere you shall hear from me. The missus desires to be kindly remembered. Nothing new about Honor—the man is a brute. Ta-ta, old fellow, and believe me yours truly,

" F. NORCOTT."

Arthur, after making himself master of the contents of this flippant epistle, stood for a moment like one turned, after the manner of Lot's wife of old, into a statue.

"When did they go?" he said at last. "I came by appointment; this must have been quite a sudden start. G——! 1 can't understand it! Gone, do you say? Impossible!"

Miss Lydia sniggered conceitedly at this assertion.

"The Colonel never came back at all," she said; "he sent for Mrs. Norcott—or else they'd settled it between them afore, which missus she thinks they did. Any way, Mrs. Norcott she packed up, and paid all that was owing the first thing this morning, and by two o'clock she was off, and missus, she had the bill put up at onst."

To this short but lucid explanation Arthur listened as one who heareth not. The melancholy truth that he had—in vulgar parlance—been *done* was beginning to dawn upon his mind. That Fred Norcott—base and unprincipled as he suspected him to be—could have the unparalleled audacity to deny and ignore the fact of his (Arthur's) ownership of the Derby winner was, however, almost too wonderful to be true. His estimate of Honor Beacham's father, though about as low a one as it is possible for one person to entertain

about another, did nevertheless fall short of believing this man capable of actual felony. That
he had trusted him so completely—had confided
so entirely in the honour of his associate, was alone
a sufficient proof that he did not consider Fred
Norcott to be capable of an act of fraud. The
transfer of Rough Diamond from Arthur's ownership to the nominal possession of the quondam
cavalry officer had been made in a decidedly loose
and unbusiness-like manner—the very nature of
the transaction necessitating to a certain extent this
unsatisfactory mode of proceeding. There was
a secret to be kept—a secret which was of vital
importance to the well-being of one of the con-
tracting parties—and therefore it followed that
" all things" were not, on this occasion, " done
decently and in order."

The suspicion, that was destined gradually to
become a settled belief in Arthur's mind, that the
man in whose power he knew himself to be was
a villain of the least creditable die, was anything
but agreeable. Pondering on this certainty, he,
as he sauntered with lingering steps towards the
splendid home which, in right of his wife, he
called his own, felt about as unhappy a young
aristocrat as ever trod the broad flagstones of
the Tyburnian pavement. His furious indignation
against the rascal by whom he had been deceived

passes the bounds of description. Had Fred Norcott chanced at that moment to present himself
within his reach, there is no saying to what
lengths the passion of the younger man might
have led him. But happily the Colonel—his faithful wife by his side, his ill-gotten gains in his
pocket, and his unrepented sins upon his head—
was far away by that time—far away to the land
where roguery is at a premium, and cheating is
dignified by the agreeable name of " smartness"—
to the land where to be a villain is no disgrace,
and where every sin save that of failure is con-
doned and pardoned.

" Now, Atty, let me look at you again—I
am sure that something is the matter—*quite* sure.
Daddy dear, doesn't Arthur look worried? And
he *will* go out so early. I thought you *would* stay
just a tiny half-hour till I have had my arrowroot,
but—"

" Stay, dear—of course I will, if you wish it,"
Arthur replied in answer to his wife's appeal,
spoken in the low and feeble voice which made
her faintest wish a law.

" I *was* going out on business, but I can put
it off till the afternoon," and he tried to speak as
if the sacrifice were no sacrifice, and as if acting
the part of deputy sick-nurse was quite in the

usual course of events for a young man about town, who had but lately completed his twenty-second year.

Sophy was, as I have said, the least selfish of human beings—she would at all times have been ready to make any sacrifice for those she loved; but a young heiress smiling over her first-born babe may be pardoned if for once in her life she failed to see that her exacting wishes militated against those of her husband, and if, while she rejoiced over the happy consciousness of his devotion, she forgot that he might have other duties to perform and other interests at stake than the one to which her entreaty had devoted him.

It was late in the afternoon before Arthur Vavasour, seizing the opportunity of a sound sleep into which the invalid had fallen, stole from the pretty morning-room adjoining that where his wife lay, stepping softly; for old Duberly—who dearly loved, after the fashion of the aged, to *talk* —might, had he heard his step upon the stairs, have intercepted his departure, and, slipping his bald head out of the half-opened study-door, have chained him—an unwilling listener—for an hour at least, in the close and stuffy atmosphere of his private sanctum.

At that moment, with his brain positively whirling with suppressed excitement, and with

the fever caused by anxiety and suspense boiling
in his veins, Arthur felt that, had he been stopped
by his respected father on his outward way, he
would have been capable of laying violent hands
upon that well-meaning but officious personage.
To rush into the fresh air—to throw himself into
a passing hansom—to be carried as fast as wheels
could bear him to the first emporium of sporting
news where he was likely to obtain authentic intelligence regarding the respective fates of Rough
Diamond and the Colonel—were the ends that
Arthur Vavasour had in view while stepping on
tiptoe down the broad stone staircase, with a
flushed face, and a heart that beat fast with long-
controlled emotion. The heaviness that had endured through the night (for, for the first time in
his life, Arthur had been kept awake by care) was
not succeeded by the joy which "cometh in the
morning," and—during the weary hours that he
had passed, book in hand, on the luxurious sofa,
among the pretty and expensive nicknacks which
adorned his wife's boudoir—the heir to countless
thousands had given himself up to the most disastrous convictions regarding his future fate. To
his then thinking—and he too soon discovered that
his forebodings had not overstepped the truth
—it seemed the most probable of misfortunes
that Frederick Norcott, taking advantage of the

carelessly-effected contract regarding the Derby
colt, had shamelessly appropriated to his own
use the proceeds of the sale of that invaluable
animal. That the man who had sunk so deep in
the mire of infamy would hesitate a moment to
make merchandise of the secret which he was well
aware his dupe and victim was keenly desirous to
preserve, Arthur could neither hope nor believe.
He was in the power—poor young fellow!—(and
miserably did he shudder under the disgraceful
yoke)—of one of the most unprincipled genteel
villains that ever walked about in well-made boots
and broadcloth, and—a grievance for the moment
still more keenly felt—his debts of honour—those
debts which he had hoped and intended by the
sale of the Derby winner to discharge—would still
remain unpaid, whilst he, under the cloud which
his own folly had gathered above his head, must
endure, with such patience as he could muster, the
consequences of a bad man's guilt.

It took but little time, and a very few inquiries,
to make sure of the fact that Colonel Norcott, with
whom no respectable sporting man (a degradation
of which Arthur was ignorant, so blind had his
passion for Honor made him) would bet—it took
but little time, I say, to make sure of the, at
first, only floating news, to wit, that the nominal owner of Rough Diamond, after securing the

amount paid by Lord Penshanger for that illustrious animal, had left England for foreign parts. Where he had gone, no one appeared able to divulge; nor did the ascertaining of the chosen spot to which he had betaken himself appear a matter of importance to the greatest sufferer by Colonel Norcott's disappearance. Arthur knew enough of law to be convinced that, even were it possible for him to brave the consequences of irritating Fred's not-over-placable disposition, the law could in this case do little or nothing towards the recovery of the stolen cash. It was horribly provoking—annoying to a scarcely endurable extent, and the more unendurable from the circumstance that to no human being could he venture to pour forth the history of his wrongs; but there was, alas, no help for it. If it should ever chance that his lucky stars might place him within arm's-reach of the " swindler," whose real character was now laid bare before him, why, then—and Arthur (who was the man to keep such an oath both to the letter and in the spirit) swore a vow between his clenched teeth, that if Frederick Norcott left his hands alive, it was about as much as that ignoble personage could reasonably expect.

CHAPTER XV.

MISFORTUNES NEVER COME SINGLY.

On his return home, two hours later, and after gleaning all the slender information in his power regarding the proceedings of his enemy, Arthur —his pocket full of certain ugly-looking letters which he had found to his address at the Travellers'—was in anything but a quietly-domestic frame of mind. With the exception of Honor— whose lovely eyes, as he had last seen them, tearful and full of piteous pleading—the idea of contact with no single human creature with whom he was connected afforded him the slightest pleasure. On the contrary, the thought of his young wife, ready, longing even to throw her weak white arms round his neck, was positively distasteful to him; the prospect of listening to old Dub's paternal twaddle he turned from with disgust; whilst the feeble cry of his one-day old heir-apparent was likely to awaken no responsive feelings in his agitated breast. On the whole, the state of feeling

in which Arthur Vavasour found himself on that
bright May afternoon may be described as a reckless one.   He was soured, discontented, almost
despairing.   Lines of care were deepening on his
brow, and it needed not the fresh blow that
awaited him in Hyde-park-terrace to convince
Arthur Vavasour that he was doomed to misfortune, and marked out for a large share of the
miseries to which flesh is heir.

" A letter that looks like business," Mr. Du-
berley said, as his son-in-law opened a missive of
large dimensions, sealed with a big seal, and altogether portentous of aspect.   " From the lawyers,"
continued the old man, " ain't it ?"

Mr. Duberly took a great and very natural
interest in the law-suit which was in progress
between Lady Millicent Vavasour and her next
heir.   He did not like, or, rather, he did positively
dislike the haughty woman who had never treated
him with the simple civility due from one educated
individual to another, and who now, in old Dub's
opinion, was conducting herself not only with a
very blamable absence of natural motherly feeling,
but with what the good man considered in the
light of something very like dishonesty.   According to his old-fashioned ideas, the will of a dead man
was a sacred thing, a document not to be lightly
set aside, and, above all, not to be set aside for

reasons of cupidity, self-interest, or love of power on the part of the pleader. In his opinion there were stringent and reciprocal duties, binding alike the parent and the child; and that foolish, prejudiced old Dub could as little understand Lady Millicent's conduct towards her offspring, as he could excuse her disrespectful and aggressive acts as regarded the dead earl her father.

Without being possessed of any inordinate fondness for wealth, Andrew Duberly was nevertheless keenly desirous that Lady Millicent should not succeed in the difficult and arduous task that she had undertaken. He was entirely ignorant of the points of law which might or might not be brought to bear favourably on her case, and was well aware that, in the event of her obtaining judgment in her favour, Arthur's mother would certainly not be inclined to treat her eldest son with any marked liberality. But it was not for that cause—or, rather, to be entirely honest—it was not for that cause only, that Andrew Duberly hoped and trusted that Earl Gillingham's will should remain *in statu quo*, and that milady should, to use his own expression, be pulled down a peg from the high horse she was so fond of mounting. The real reason for the fervour of zeal into which he had worked himself might be sought for, however, as is so often the case, in personal motives. Lady

Millicent had wounded and mortified both himself and the child he loved; which being the case, it was only natural that the old millionaire, excellent Christian though he was, should have viewed with complacency the possible chances of her discomfiture.

"Well?" said Mr. Duberly interrogatively, for the terms on which he lived with his son-in-law warranted the reality as well as the appearance of curiosity,—"well, what says the enemy? We're never going to say die, eh? I'll tell you what, Arthur; rather than that, I'd pay five thousand pounds for you to the lawyers—five thousand! I'd pay ten to help keep your rights. It isn't the money, but the principle that I think so much of. But, I say, what *does* the old quill-driver write to you about? Let's see the letter; or if you'd rather not, I—"

"O no, sir; take it. It isn't that, but it's all such a beastly bore. You see he says that Houndsford's opinion is against my chance; and if it is, what's the use of not giving in? I don't like the scandal of the thing, fighting a case against one's own mother; and—"

"Stuff and nonsense, boy; it's milady's doing, and not yours. It's *her* that's setting it all a-going; and if you'll take my advice, you'll not give in till you're obliged to. However, there's time enough to talk of that by and by. Sophy's

been asking for you more than once, poor girl,
whilst you was away; and as for the boy, he's
been holloring like a good 'un. *His* lungs are
sound enough, at any rate, bless him!" And
" grandpapa," after fixing his gold spectacles once
more upon his nose, returned to the perusal of the
newspaper, in which his soul delighted.

Perhaps among the minor difficulties of social
life there are none which are more often or more
painfully felt than that almost insurmountable one
of concealing from the watchful eyes of affection
the heavy cares and inward anxieties from which
we may be suffering. By the weaker sex, who
are trained from infancy to the art of hiding their
feelings under the cloak of reticence and decorum,
the task is comparatively an easy one. Almost
unconsciously, and as an affair of habit, they daily
practise it, till practice makes perfect, and art becomes to them a second, and sometimes a more
winning and graceful nature. But with men it is
widely different. Even the best performers among
them are apt to forget, to stumble over, or to
overact their parts; and though they may sometimes succeed in deceiving one of their own sex,
it rarely happens that the least observant of the
other does not possess the moderate clear-sightedness requisite to lay a finger on the truth at
once.

Conscious as he was of this masculine imper-
fection, and well aware that he could not keep up
before his wife the appearance of a contentment
which he was far from feeling, it was a relief to
Arthur that the autocratic guardian of his wife's
health—the stout, somniferous lady, who looked
the higher order of monthly nurse all over—ob-
jected strongly to any conversation taking place
between her patient and the inexperienced young
husband, who was " so attentive, bless you," as
she said afterwards to the Mrs. Harris of her
elevated sphere, and who was " one of the best
of 'usbands to the nicest young lady she had ever
nussed."

Nor did Sophy, in her " mother's prime of
bliss," desire and crave for more than the privilege of looking at her well-loved Arthur's handsome face, of pressing very softly and tenderly
the dear hand that held her own, and of murmur-
ing into his bent-down ear that she was very,
very happy.

" Isn't he a darling?" she whispered, alluding to the precious object of her new-found hopes;
" I am sure—quite sure, though nurse said he
didn't—that he looked at me just now. You can
see his dear little face. There !" And that Arthur might enjoy this privilege, the happy young
creature turned away a few inches of the bed-

covering, gazing down the while with touching fondness on her sleeping treasure.

And Arthur—who really was goodnatured, and who, but for the anxieties and annoyances which were oppressing him, would probably have been almost as contented and joyous as herself—did his best to seem interested in the small atom of humanity which he could hardly bring himself to believe he had the right to call his son; but smile and flatter tenderly as he might, Sophy, with the intuitive perception that love alone can give, heard a something in his voice which told her that all was not as it should be with the father of her child.

"Now, Atty," she said, pressing his hand to her soft lips, "you have been teased and worried again, I know you have, by something or somebody. It isn't poor papa, is it, dear? I daresay he is tiresome, poor old man, just now; but you musn't mind. It is all so new to him, you know, and he thinks baby such a wonderful thing."

"Well, and so he is," Arthur said with a smile, which quite reassured the young mother, who was so willing to see everything *en rose*, "and your father is a brick, and doesn't bore me the least in life. What made you fancy such nonsense, you foolish child? O, I'm to go, am I? I wish we had you downstairs again, dear. The governor and I miss you dreadfully at dinner. By Jove, there's the bell, and I haven't even washed my hands—all your fault, Fee," and he left her with the memory of another kiss to brighten her hours of silence.

Poor, gentle, unsuspicious Sophy! She little guessed the troubled heart, the wearisomeness of spirit, on which the door of that spacious chamber closed when Arthur Vavasour went out from her presence. She loved the man who only liked, respected, *cared* for her, with a passion almost equal to *his* for the beautiful woman of whose very existence the trusting wife had ceased to think; loved him with a love which was rapidly superseding, crushing, nay well-nigh annihilating with its rapid and luxuriant growth the lowlier flowerets of a daughter's tenderness — flowerets that had grown with her growth and strengthened with her strength till such time as the stronger seed was sown, the produce of which was destined, according to the law of nature, to suppress, if not indeed actually to destroy, the weaker herbage amongst which it had chanced to take root and flourish. Already was this girl, the child of a doting father, apologising for and more than half-regretting the presence of that father in the home which the old man's excessive fondness for herself might render less agreeable to her husband; already she was giving to Arthur proofs, open and unrestrained, that he, and he alone, reigned paramount in her affections; and could the loving old man, to whom she was all in all, have looked into the young heart he thought he knew so well, the father would have learned there some very bitter truths. For the ignorance that was bliss to him, Andrew Duberly paid afterwards a heavy price. The wish to believe in what rendered him a happy man was father to the joyful thought that in his daughter's affections her young and handsome husband held but a secondary place, and in that belief old Dub continued to his dying hour. But a day of reckoning—a day which, in the full flush, in the almost fever of his prime of bliss, the millionaire was far as are the poles asunder from anticipating—was, alas, very near at hand! The day of retribution for time misspent and wasted, for wealth abused, for golden opportunities neglected, for benefits unthankfully enjoyed, for—to sum up all—the myriad sins which render it no easy thing for a rich man to enter into the kingdom of heaven. Yes, the day of retribution for the minor and unnoticed sins of this "just man" was near at hand; but in the mean time not a care oppressed him, nor did a single foreboding of evil to come mar his keen enjoyment of the present.

The game at picquet with Arthur, who, poor

fellow, was all the while wishing his father-in-law, if not exactly in his grave, at least a hundred miles away, was played by this light-hearted grandpapa with a zest and spirit which set Arthur (who was at that time taking rather a gloomy view of human life) wondering how any man in his senses could have lived to the age of three-score years and ten without having arrived at the conclusion that all things (including a dull game with painted pasteboard) here below are, with no single exception, only vanity and vexation of spirit.

CHAPTER XVI.

OUT AT SEA.

THE sun rose bright and cloudless on the day following Honor's return; and John Beacham, whose hands were, as usual, brimful of business, and who moreover had decided, after a short consultation with himself, that his womankind were more likely to come to a good understanding without him, betook himself, immediately after breakfast, to the hay-fields, which were ripe for the scythe, and only waited the master's fiat to lie in promising swaths upon the rich meadow-land which called John Beacham owner.

Honor saw him depart with a weary sigh. The prospect of a lengthened *téte-à-téte* with the stern old lady, whose brow never relaxed for a passing moment from its rigidity, and who had not even vouchsafed a distant "good-morning" in answer to her civil greeting, was a penance which it almost made her blood run cold to think of. Her own courage—the temporary boldness

which was the offspring of hurt feeling and great
but temporary excitement—had oozed out either
at the ends of her taper fingers, or with the tears
with which she had watered her morning pillow.
When she found herself alone with her dreaded
foe, poor Honor had not—as the saying goes—a
word to throw at a dog; she was in the mood to cry
her eyes out, and in the temper to long earnestly
for pity and tenderness. One kind and encouraging
word, one look even of sympathy, would have
brought the poor thing on her knees before her
natural enemy, and all might have been well between the pair whom God had joined together in
bonds that nought save sin could sever.

For three days—three miserable days—during
which John, engrossed by business cares, and
hoping, as sanguine men in spite of appearances
will, that all would come right at last, appeared to
take no notice of the silence only broken by sarcastic speeches, and by the "talking at" (which
to some women is a positive accomplishment) on
his mother's part, which reigned between her and
Honor—during those three miserable days, the
seeds destined to produce very bitter fruit were
being sown with terrible certainty in Honor
Beacham's breast. She was the last woman in
the world to endure without evil consequences
the description of torture to which she was being

subjected. Fond of popularity—eager to be loved
—impulsive—passionate if you will, this girl, who
could only be what she called angry for a passing
moment, would, for anyone who, to use her own
expression, have been "kind to her," have been
the most docile and tenderest of friends and de-
pendents.

But unfortunately—*most* unfortunately, as the
sequel will prove—it was not in Mrs. Beacham's
nature to forgive. She believed herself to be a
Christian; she thought, so little did she know her
own feelings, that she harboured neither malice
nor hatred in her heart, but all the while there
was scarcely a harder (and certainly there could
scarcely be a harder *seeming*) idiosyncrasy than
that which was owned by this *soi-disant* believer in
the Christian faith. Mercy for Honor—pity for the
wicked wife who had shown herself so false and
flighty—she had none. The pale delicate face,
bending over her woman's-work, appealed to this
unrelenting woman's heart in vain. The days—
even suppposing them ever to have existed—when
Mrs. Beacham knew what temptation was, had
long since passed away, and were forgotten; all
she remembered was that *she* had through all her
married life been blameless, industrious, and submissive, and that these virtues endowed her with
the right to be the judge and condemner of others

was neither to be removed nor shaken. Poor Honor, poor little impressionable, impulsive girl! Her spirits felt very heavy, and her heart beat with almost painful quickness when, on the fourth morning after her compulsory return, Mrs. Beacham brought her work (it was her first time of doing so) and established herself alarmingly near to the broad old-fashioned window-seat, Honor's favorite and accustomed working-place. Dragging after her the big sheet on which she was about to perform the housewifely operation of "turning," her tortoiseshell spectacles fixed on her keen hawk-like nose, John's mother did indeed appear in the light of a terrible object to her timid and easily-subdued daughter-in-law. Honor did not possess (and well she knew her weakness) the courage requisite for self-defence; and during the short period of silence which followed on Mrs. Beacham's establishment of herself in front of her own special little work-table, Honor, had she dared, would gladly have taken flight, and betaking herself to her room, have there waited in silence and solitude for her husband's return. But to make this move required an amount of hardihood of which poor Honor was utterly incapable. She felt entirely subdued — oppressed beyond the power of description, by the very presence of her mother-in-law. Whatever resolutions — whatever

plans of resistance she might have formed whilst
alone, or in the presence only of her husband,
faded away entirely when those light-gray, aged,
but still penetrating eyes were fixed upon her,
and when she knew with the intuition of fear that
Mrs. Beacham was about to give her what is vulgarly called a " piece of her mind."

The dreaded exordium began after this fashion :

" When you was a child, Mrs. John," the old
lady said, pushing up her spectacles and peering
at Honor through her half-closed eyelids—" when
you was a child, did you get any Bible learning?
and was anybody good enough to teach you your
catechism ?"

" They were," Honor replied, opening her large
blue eyes in wonder, and using, to the old lady's
disgust, the peculiar Irish form of assent which,
singularly enough, seemed indigenous in this girl
who had had so little experience of her father-
land—" they were ;" and then she stopped, poor
child, marvelling greatly to what these singular
opening questions were about to lead.

" Well, then," continued Mrs. Beacham, spread-
ing out two bony hands in simulated horror, " all
I can say is, that *I* can see *no* excuse for you.
If, besides being what I won't defile my lips by
naming, you had been turned out into the streets,
as many of them creatures are, without eddication,

and without knowing how to read your Bible, 1 *might* have, and so might John have, passed over something; but when a gell has been taught her dooty, and, more than that, when a gentleman as *is* respectable is good enough to make an honest woman of her, all I can say is, that when she can behave as you have done, when she can lie and deceive, and act light with other men, why she ought — and there ain't a decent person that wouldn't say as much—she ought to be ashamed of herself!"

To this coarse attack Honor vouchsafed no reply. The violence of invective employed by the determined old woman positively stunned her. The only feeling of which she was at all conscious was one of anger, of anger stirred up by grievous words in as gentle a breast as ever belonged to woman. The silence with which her words were received was very irritating to the speaker. She had looked forward, with very considerable satisfaction, to the moment when she should overwhelm her recreant daughter-in-law with a fire of well-merited reproaches; and now, to her infinite annoyance, her shots seemed to miss fire, and not a single one was returned as a proof that the volley had in any way been felt by the enemy.

"If anyone had told me," the old lady went on to say, speaking very calmly and deliberately now, and as if determined that every word should tell—" if anyone had told me, fifteen months ago, that my son's wife would bring his family—*my* family, that is to say, that has lived respectable time out of mind—to disgrace, I wouldn't, no, *I wouldn't* have believed it ! It's the first time (though I say it, as perhaps shouldn't) that a Turton or a Beacham has numbered such a one as you among them ; and I never thought to live to see the day when folks could point at one as bears my name, and even her to a wanton !"

The word was out at last, the ugly shocking word that struck through Honor's brain like a knife, and which, when it had passed the lips that spoke it, the irritated woman, when it was too late, possibly wished unsaid. In very truth, there was something startling in the sight of Honor's livid face and flashing eyes, something almost painful even to the unsympathising witness of her agony in the change which a few outspoken syllables had wrought in that young girl's countenance.

Rising suddenly from her chair, tossing aside with reckless hand the woman's-work with which she had been occupied, her pretty taper fingers pressed against her throat (for there was a tightening there that felt like suffocation), Honor Beacham stood erect before her stepmother.

" You are wicked!" she stammered forth. " A wicked, cruel woman ! John would not have used me so—John knows I do not deserve such words. I will go to him—to my husband—I will—"

" You will do nothing of the kind. If you do not know your duty, I must teach it to you," almost shrieked the passionate old woman, losing all command over herself, as the idea of Honor's appealing to John against his mother presented itself to her mind. " You think, do you, that John—that *my* son is going to indulge you in all your good-for-nothing ways? Why, girl, he said to me himself that it was high time something was done to bring milady to her senses ; he said—"

But Honor—nervous, excited, and scarcely mistress of her actions—waited to hear no more. With a cry like that of a hare hard pressed by the hounds, she rushed from the room, leaving the startled old woman to ponder with some trepidation on the mischief she had wrought. Long, and not very comfortably, did she think over her words ; but after a considerable amount of putting two and two together, and no little leaning towards herself as an oracle to be respected, the balance of opinion being on the whole decidedly in favour of her own proceedings, Mrs. Beacham arrived at the conclusion that she was fully justified in speaking as she had done to the erring Honor. Judging that strong-minded woman according to the average truthfulness of her sex, John's respected parent could not, on the whole, be accused, while quoting John's indignant words, of the sin of mendacity. According to the letter of those words, she was justified in repeating as a fact her son's awful threat—the one which more than any other of her angry vituperations had told upon Honor's feelings— the threat, namely, that her husband would, instigated thereto by his mother, bring his pretty young wife " to her senses."

There was something very vague and terrible in this menace; and Honor, after locking the door of the pretty bedroom which John, little more than one short year before, had taken such pleasure in making ready for his darling, brooded over them with a sick heart and miserably. She was utterly in the dark, as I have already and more than once endeavoured to explain, regarding her husband's character generally, and his feelings towards herself in particular. Could any-one at that particular moment—when she was brooding over her wrongs—over her husband's coldness of heart and heat of temper; over his cruelty in delivering her over to the tormentor, *id est,* the mother who bore him, and her own misery in being condemned to live *en tiers* with two people who disliked and despised her—had anyone, I repeat, at that especial moment whispered in Honor Beacham's ear that John the *incompris* possessed in reality the very tenderest of hearts; that his apparent coldness towards herself was the result of a keen sense of personal and educational inferiority; and that a few sweet smiles on her dear lips, and a few kind loving words whispered in his ear, would make poor John not only the happiest, but the most demonstrative of husbands, Honor would simply have told that well-intentioned comforter that he knew not what he said, and, turning on her restless pillow, would have sternly refused to credit the fact that she was otherwise than a victim.

I fear me much that the behaviour of Honor at this crisis of her life will find few to excuse it; and yet to the thinking of the lenient there will be found some plausible reasons for her folly. In the first place, she was both mentally and bodily out of health. Of neither truths, patent though they were, had she any real or wholesome suspicion. She was too young, too ignorant of cause and effect, to be aware that the life she had been leading had thrown her into a mental fever, the which, seeing that it was a malady of weakness, required the nicest care and the most judicious of treatments in order to effect its cure. Neither could she give a name to the *malaise*, showing itself in languor, in nervous headaches, and in occasional heart-palpitations; all of which, with the carelessness so common to the young, she had hitherto allowed to pass unnoticed. That she was in no frame, either of mind or body, to do battle successfully against the violence of her own feelings and forebodings is very certain; and as certain is it that, though she did not yet what is called *love* the man who had conspired so selfishly against her peace, the image and the memory of Arthur Vavasour formed no small portion of her troubled thoughts, as she lay sobbing on her bed, and repeating to herself that she could not, would not bear the lot that lay before her.

"To the old," as someone—I know not who —has truthfully said, "sorrow is sorrow, while to the young it is despair." Despair at least as they to whom sorrow is new count the extreme of human suffering. The smallest insect, as the inspired poet tells us, " feels a pang as great as when a giant dies;" and Honor, frail little vessel as she was, could, she believed, endure no heavier or more wearing woe than that of submitting in her fresh young beauty—the beauty that Arthur

Vavasour worshipped — to the tyranny of her mother-in-law, and the cold displeasure of a husband who loved her not.

As she dwelt—with the pleasure which under twenty is so often felt in the indulgence of a mournful self-pity—on her unmitigated woes, the idea, once before entertained, and never wholly forgotten, of finding a home for herself—of working for her bread—of escaping from the tyranny, the evil-speaking, the taunts and evil suspicions of her mother-in-law, flashed through her mind. At first, with something very like a shock—for to Honor the leaving of her husband's house and home appeared (distinction without a difference though it was) a far more adventurous and desperate act than that which she had before, with tolerable calmness, contemplated—the act, that is to say, of separating herself whilst under her father's roof from the husband who, in her opinion, neither loved, appreciated, nor understood her; from the man who could see her wronged, insulted, and put upon by the hard-tempered old woman, who, from the hour of her introduction to Updown Paddocks, had never ceased to make Honor's life a misery and a burden to her;— the act and deed of remaining hidden in some obscure London lodging, had, as I said before, seemed simple and easy enough to the young wife when, encouraged and buoyed-up by the devoted attentions of Arthur Vavasour, she vaguely contemplated a future in which Mrs. Beacham had no share, but which was to be cheered by the unfailing friendship (Honor knew so little of men's nature that she had faith in constancy, and dreamed of friendship as a delicious possibility) of her kind and disinterested adviser. But the prospect before her was a trifle changed by the point of view from which she now contemplated it; and far greater courage and strength of mind seemed required to induce her to leave her husband's home than had been needed to enable her to stay away from it. As her fever of passion cooled, so did the power within her to take a step so decided and so desperate fade away likewise. Honor's nature was naturally an indolent one—indolent and yielding. Should she be led, by the force of her own rebellious temper, to do that which would blight her name and ruin her hopes of future happiness, the guilt of that act would lie—as such guilts so often do— more at the door of another than at her own. Already the quiet tears of self-pity and womanly submission were taking the place of hysterical sobs and passionate ejaculations; already she was subsiding into the dull calm which is the natural consequence of over-excitement, when the voice, harsh-sounding and dreaded, of the domestic tyrant—

whose will had grown to be law, and whose ways
were not as the ways of her young daughter-in-
law—smote suddenly on Honor's sensitive ear,
and awoke again within her the evil spirit of
resistance. Mrs. Beacham was only, at that un-
lucky moment, in the exercise of her right; she
was but scolding the girl-of-all-work, the female
" odd boy" of the establishment, for some trifling
neglect of her multifarious duties; but the evil
done by that loud high-pitched voice was as surely
effected, and its baneful influence on the listener's
mind was as great and fatal, as though the most
inexcusable deed of injustice and cruelty had been
then and there by John's hasty-tempered parent
committed. Rising in a sitting posture on her
bed, Honor, with shaking fingers, pushed the hair
back from her aching forehead, and repeating to herself more than once, as if in excuse for her pre-
meditated sin, that she could not, could not bear
her life at Updown, she slowly slid down her feet
upon the floor, and (half mechanically at first)
commenced her preparations for departure. For
departure? Yes; but to what place, and with what
ulterior end, she knew not. All she cared for was
escape—escape from the sight and sound of the
woman who had always hated her, and who, as
Honor firmly believed, had begun to undermine
her husband's love and trust, and would even-

tually succeed in turning his heart against her.
To live any longer under the same roof with one
who had accused her of the vilest sin—who had
reproached her in the coarsest terms, for acts of
which she was utterly incapable—was, as Honor
kept repeating to herself, more than she could
endure. *More* unhappy, the foolish child believed
she could not be. It might be hard, trying at
first, and humiliating, to work as a servant, or in
other ways, for her bread; but anything, to her
then thinking, was better than her present life;
and Arthur Vavasour—(it is to be feared that, innocent though in truth she was, that young gentleman played rather a conspicuous part in the pro-
gramme of her future plans)—Arthur Vavasour
would be ever at hand to aid, advise, and encourage her. On one subject only did Honor from
the first, and wholly without reservation, make
up her disturbed and rather bewildered mind.
She would not, under any circumstances, take
refuge under her father's roof. That John would
immediately commence the strictest search to discover her whereabouts Honor was well assured,
and therefore it was above all things necessary
for the preservation of her secret, that in Stanwick-street they should know positively nothing of
her proceedings.

The only individual—alas, for this poor silly

girl—this frail, weak vessel about to put to sea
without a pilot, and with no chart or compass to
guide it on its way—the only individual to whom
the mystery of her setting sail on her adventurous
cruise was to be no mystery, was the last person
in the world to whom she should have confided the
secrets of her life. To Arthur Vavasour—to the
man whose " brotherly" kindness (he had been
very cautious in his love-making of late, and
Honor had in consequence grown proportionally
off her guard)—to Arthur Vavasour only would
she at once apply in this emergency for counsel
and support. From him, she was well assured,
she would never fail to meet with gentleness and
respect. When she looked back upon his de-
ferential manner—on his unceasing *kindness*, as
Honor in her simplicity considered it—above all,
when she compared that kindness and that defer-
ence with the aggressive treatment which from
John's unendurable parent had so greatly angered
her, and also with the absence, for reasons which
she knew not, of demonstrative affection from her
husband—it is scarcely matter for surprise that
Honor Beacham should have loved and cherished
the man who gave to her—such was her woman's
faith—the offering which she prized the most;
the offering, that is to say, of an affection on
which, through evil report and through good re-

port, and while life should last, she could con-
fidently rely.

Honor Beacham would have been no true woman if she had not, before making the first commonplace preparations for flight (which, of course,
she being *pro tem.* a heroine, included counting
out the money, and putting on the inevitable
cloak and bonnet), written a few lines to an-
nounce her resolution to the person whom she
deemed, in her insane delusion, to be the most
deeply interested therein.   There is something, to
many of the softer sex, very reassuring in wielding
that dangerous instrument of feeble woman, the
one to which it is so fatally easy in moments of
passionate excitement to have recourse—to wit,
the pen; and Honor, with the following note written, stamped, and ready for posting in her pocket,
felt far more prepared than she had done (previous to its production) for the difficulties and
dangers with which her path was strewed :

"DEAR MR. VAVASOUR,—I am afraid you will
think me foolish" (Honor did not entertain any
such alarm, but the sentence appeared to her in
the light of the proper thing, so she allowed it to
stand), "but since my return home—which was
very sudden, as Mr. Beacham would not even
allow me to say good-bye to my father—I have

been made too unhappy and too angry to stay here any longer. It is not so much because of my husband, who would be good to me if he was allowed, but on account of old Mrs. Beacham, who has grown crosser than ever, and who quite hates me now, I am sure. I would bear it if I could, but I cannot; so to-day I go up to London, and shall soon, I hope, get a place of some kind through your help. I should like to be nursery governess best, as I was before, at the Clays', and should like to begin directly, as I have not much money. I shall be called Honor Blake, as I was before; and John will know nothing, any more than my father or other friends, excepting you, where I am. When I am in London, I will write again to you, to say where I am. Please to burn this; and believe, with a great many thanks, that I am your grateful friend,

"HONOR BEACHAM.

"P.S.—I was so sorry to leave the play; you will tell me when we meet how it ended."

After writing this letter, the child of impulse by whom it was penned felt, for the time requisite to perfect her arrangements, equal to any emergency. With the letter directed to Arthur Vavasour in her pocket, a something of his actual presence seemed to support and strengthen her.

That letter, she doubted not, would bring joy—
not guilty joy—that, to do her only justice, Honor
never suspected—to the heart that desired her
happiness, and was glad to sun itself in her presence. That any wrong was done to the trusting
wife of her friend, by that friend's kindly feelings
towards herself, Honor was innocent of imagining. She believed in this young man's virtuous
attachment, and gratefully enjoyed the comfort
of her convictions.

The hardest task which she had to perform
—for she could not wholly divest herself of the
idea that John, in his blundering, unattractive
way, did cherish, and would for a time grieve
over her loss—was the inditing of a farewell missive to her husband. Two attempts did she make
ere she could express in a few words the con-
tradictory sentiments which caused, in spite of herself, the tears to fall over the paper, and which
made the pen with which she wrote look misty between her agitated fingers. At last the painful
duty was over, and the words that were so soon
to shake the frame of the strong man who read
them like a reed, ran as follows :

" DEAR JOHN,—I hope you will forgive me for
not being able to stay at the Paddocks any longer.
I could have lived with you, and perhaps have

been happy; for I know you are good, and you would not have been hard upon my silliness. What drives me away I leave it to yourself to guess. I have had a good deal to bear; but what hurt me the most was your mother telling me that you meant to be hard upon me too. Do not, please, try to find out where I am. I shall go into service, and try to keep an honest name, though your mother says I have brought disgrace on hers. I should like to think that you forgave me, John. Perhaps I shall some day; or I may not till we are both in another world, where I pray that we may meet, and that you may be happier without me than they say I have made you here. I cannot keep from crying over this letter; for, John, we might have been happy, if only your mother had not had bad thoughts of me from the beginning. God bless you, John; and believe that I am your foolish, but not your wicked wife, as your mother says I am,

"Honor Beacham."

By the time that this letter was finished it wanted but an hour of noon (they kept old farm-house hours at the Paddocks), and the striking by the big hall - clock of the time o' day warned Honor that if she wished to catch a certain train that touched, on its way to London, for a few minutes at the small station of Switcham, she must waste no more time, either in thinking over her plans, or in making ready for her journey. Accordingly, with a steadiness which, under the circumstances, was surprising, she put together a very few articles of dress — and leaving behind her the simple ornaments, poor John's wedding-gifts—over which she was so little of a heroine that she heaved a faint sigh of regret—this wife of little more than a year left the shelter of her husband's roof, and, apparently with the intention of taking one of the quiet country walks to which she was accustomed, sauntered slowly, till she was out of sight of the Peartree-house occupants, across the fields that lay between them and the village.

Once the station reached, she cared little either for notice or discovery. The desperate step she had taken could not long remain a secret from the neighbourhood at large ; but by the time that John received her letter, she would—according to her present expectations—be already lost to him, and far beyond reach of discovery, in some well-chosen but, of course, very humble retreat, which Arthur Vavasour's thoughtful kindness would, she doubted not, speedily provide for her. With her mind full of these projects, but with a heart only half rejoicing over her newly-found freedom, Honor

went on her way. Her head ached, and a strange
sense of weariness rendered her steps slow and
lagging; but, for all that she both felt and looked
ill, there was about her air and walk (her face
was too hidden by a thick veil for strangers'
eyes to gaze upon it) that nameless charm
which commands attention, and excites the notice
of the curious. Unconscious of, and at the moment utterly indifferent to, admiration, Honor
turned her eyes neither to the right hand nor to
the left as she passed slowly along the village-
street. On her arrival at the post-office, she
dropped—without allowing herself a moment's reflection—the two letters she had written into the
box; and then feeling a little more frightened and
bewildered than she had done before—for there
was a sense of the inexorable in this apparently
unimportant act—she walked forward, erect, and
outwardly with something of defiance in her mien,
towards the station.

There may be some among my readers who
perhaps will consider that Honor's proceedings—
her intemperate conduct in thus suddenly giving
up home-ties and the respectability attendant
thereon, and her apparent absence of womanly
feeling regarding her husband — are overstrained
and unnatural. But let it be remembered that she
was young—young and inexperienced—impulsive

too, as well as a little vain and exacting. To understand the young, however, the investigator into character must be young himself. When youth has passed, we forget not only the feelings that dwelt within us in the days of the long-ago past, but the excuses for our sins and follies, which then seemed to us as sands by the sea-shore in number. We forget the craving after the storms of life, the desire to be " for ever climbing after the climbing wave," together with the loathing of sad satiety, the satiety which a quiet and unbroken existence awakens in the breast of those who are yet idle and untried enough to talk of indulging in grief, and who have still to learn the bitter truth that to endure is hard enough. Honor Beacham was so romantic and simple that she could hug to her breast the discontent which she had dignified into despair. Very like a heroine she felt as the swift train bore her onwards into the unknown regions of the future. With the sharp and scolding voice of her mother-in-law still ringing in her ears, and with the *certainty* (for Honor was of an age and nature to believe in every result she wished for) of having escaped from Mrs. Beacham's tyrannic rule, it was surely natural that she should feel a keen sense of triumph at her own success, and that an involuntary smile should flit over her lips as she thought of the old woman's face of discomfiture when the startling and unwelcome discovery would be made, that her victim was already far beyond the precincts of her power.

Of John—of the husband who, excepting in rare moments of anger, had always been kind to her, and considerate, as far as he comprehended them, of her feelings, it was not quite so pleasant to think; and Honor endeavoured to the best of her ability to put aside the obtrusive reflections connected with his probable regret by repeating to herself the scarcely-believed truth that her husband would soon forget her. "His mother is all in all to him," the young wife told herself; "had she not been, he never would have allowed me to be so tormented; and besides, he is so busy, so always, always busy;" and Honor heaved a little sigh over the enjoyment by honest John of one of the greatest blessings that can fall to the lot of any human being, whether he or she be young or old, rich or poor, gentle or simple. If idleness be, as the Book of books informs us, the root of all evil, so surely is *work*, wholesome, needful work, the surest and best safeguard against the ills of life. It is the idleness of the rich which, more than any other cause, renders it harder for them than for their fellows to "enter into the kingdom of heaven."

CHAPTER XVII.

"CONTENTMENT," to quote the words of the wisest of mankind, "is great gain;" and true enough also is often the converse of the assertion—namely, that in "discontent there is exceeding loss." In Lady Millicent Vavasour's case, however, there seemed every chance that an exception to both rules would be found; for the desire and determination to reverse a decree which angered her, and which had for years been the mainspring and motive of one of the most unwomanly of actions, seemed likely to be crowned with success. Very wonderful, as well as praiseworthy (had her motive been a nobler one), were the exertions which, quite *sub rosa*, and working like a mole beneath the soil, she had made to effect that always extremely difficult result—namely, the setting aside of an obnoxious will. The money she had spent —the fees she had paid—the consultations with eminent lawyers that she had undergone—the perseverance and clear-sightedness of which she had given proofs, were worthy, one and all, of a better cause. At last—whether it was that by her continual coming she wearied them—or whether the great law lords did really—partly incited thereto, perhaps, by the prestige enjoyed by the wealth and "standing" of the grandiose Lady Millicent—consider that she had right and justice on her side, certain it is that opinions favourable to her cause were placing Arthur Vavasour's position as heir-apparent of Gillingham in rather a precarious and unsatisfactory point of view. Between himself and his mother there had never, as we well know, existed, either on this or any other subject, any great amount either of confidence or affection; nor was it probable that the small degree of both, that it was only fair to suppose might be lying latent in those two antagonistic breasts, would be much increased and strengthened by the approaching triumph (for such all visible tokens announced it to be) of the already vain-glorious Lady Millicent.

That triumph—for such news ever travels quickly—began speedily to be noised abroad, to the annoyance of Arthur, whose creditors grew once more on the alert, and to the extreme displeasure of Mr. Duberly, whose usually placid temper would, but for his ever-increasing delight in his new toy, *i.e.* his grandson, have betrayed outward signs of discomposure and annoyance.

"I guessed how it would be, boy, all along," he said to Arthur, on the third morning after the one which had first thrown light upon the baby's tiny face; "I knew how it would be. Milady would never rest, not she, till she made her father out to be *non compos*, or some such devilment. Well, I thank my stars that we old-fashioned folks that you grandees call snobs, would be long enough before they tried-on such a thing as that comes to;" and the old man, so saying, looked as savage as it was possible for a round-faced, kindly, elderly gentleman, who was in reality brimming over with the milk of human kindness, to do.

A little to his surprise, and also, if the truth must be owned, to his disappointment, Arthur appeared not nearly so interested in this all-important matter as might have been reasonably expected. Neither while his father-in-law was giving utterance to the above very decided opinion, nor when the old gentleman, laying down the fork on which he had fixed a tempting morsel of toasted breakfast-bacon, clearly awaited a reply, did Arthur think proper to evince any tokens of a congenial spirit. The fact was (and surely the cause will be considered a sufficient one) he had

that moment received the second and promised
note from Honor, informing him of her address,
and asking him very humbly, and with none of
the old playfulness and evident sense of something
like equality between them which had character-
ised her former proceedings, whether he could in
any way assist her to gain her livelihood.   "For
I feel very forlorn and helpless," the poor girl
wrote, "and almost think that I had better have
borne with Mrs. Beacham's temper.   But it is too
late now; and if you can in any way help me, I
shall be very, very grateful for your aid."

It was with this short missive, touching in its
tone of lowliness and impuissance, safe in his
waistcoat-pocket, that Arthur, with an absent and
preoccupied air, listened to the old man's words.
That the sound of them, however, lingered in his
ear, and in some sort made their way through it
to his understanding, was evidenced by his saying
in answer to Mr. Duberly's lengthened stare of
surprise :

"I beg your pardon, sir; I was thinking of
something else.   I ought"—and his colour rose
as he told the falsehood which Honor's letter demanded of him—"I have, that is to say, to go
out this morning on business connected with this
horrid law-affair.   There is a proposal from my
man to settle it amicably, and—"

"Amicably be hanged!" cried Mr. Duberly, rising from the table in a pet. "If I was you, I wouldn't hear of being amicable; and I wonder those rascally lawyers have the face to propose such a thing."

"O, *they* have face enough for anything!" said Arthur, who was anxiously humouring the old gentleman, to keep him in a tolerably acquiescing mood. "There is nothing, sooner or later, that any one of them, if it suited his book, wouldn't propose. One has to look deuced sharp after them, I can tell you, sir; so I am off directly after breakfast to Lincoln's Inn. Any commands?" pausing at the door, which, in his anxiety to escape, he had already reached. "I shall just take a look at Sophy and the brat, and then I'm off."

"Good young fellow," Mr. Duberly muttered to himself as the sound of Arthur's footsteps died away on the marble pavement of the inner hall; and Arthur, who was well aware of the admirable impression that his last words had made, felt no shadow of remorse for the deception of which he had been guilty. Nor did his cheek tingle with tardy shame when pretty Sophy (for she did look really pretty in the delicate paleness of invalidism) called him her darling Arthur, and whispered half fearfully (she did not wish, poor child, to be troublesome) that she would not be quite happy till she saw his face again.

Glad to be released, and eager to commence with the least possible delay his new office of protector and sole friend of his beautiful Honor, Arthur, who had waited since the previous night in sleepless eagerness for his summons, bade his wife good-bye with ill-dissembled haste, and was speedily on his way to the obscure street, somewhere in the direction of the Strand, where Honor had found a temporary home. It was a narrow and certainly not an inviting-looking place that to which she in her ignorance had betaken herself. She had passed it in a four-wheeled cab on her way from the Waterloo station to—she knew not where; and reading on a bill in the front window of what looked to her inexperienced eye a respectable house, that there were lodgings to let, she desired the driver to stop, and forthwith commenced inquiries regarding the apartments in question.

The mistress of the house, a rather forbidding-looking person in a tumbled black-net cap, and just the *soupçon* of a moustache on her lip, looked slightly surprised at Honor's appearance; and at her demand whether she would receive her as an inmate, Mrs. Casey (for so was the woman called) promptly replied in the affirmative, adding irrelevantly, as Honor thought, that though her name was Irish, she was English born and bred.

"And I am Irish too," Honor said eagerly, "and my name is Blake. I am just come from the country" (there was little necessity for telling Mrs. Casey *that*), "and I know nobody—except one person," she added with a pretty blush, the suddenness of which was not lost upon her quick-sighted interlocutor—"one person who will get me a situation," she went on hurriedly—"a situation as nursery governess. I was that before; and till I get a place, I should like very much" (Honor already began to dislike the idea of wandering far afield in search of a domicile) "to stay with you."

To this request, after a slight demur on the part of the owner, or rather lessee of No. 29 Sussex-street—a demur occasioned by her unwillingness to appear over-anxious to possess her new acquaintance as a tenant—Mrs. Casey graciously acceded. The terms were not moderate —a pound per week for two very small rooms on the second story; but Honor made no objection. She was too glad to get over as well as she had done the awkward question of a reference, for any idea of bargaining to obtrude itself on her mind; and thus, in the space of little more time than it has required to scribble down this page, the bargain was concluded, and Honor Beacham, feeling very strange, and not a little lonesome, took quiet possession of her apartments.

By this time it was nearly two o'clock, and Honor, in a solitude only broken by the ceaseless roll of wheels, and by all the multifarious uproar of a crowded London thoroughfare, began, against her will, to think over what was going on at Pear-tree House. It was just possible, seeing that she and the old lady had parted on such extremely bad terms, that the latter, deeming it more dignified to leave her adversary to herself, had never even made any inquiries concerning her; and even had she done so, Honor felt no fear that any inquiries of the enemy would lead either to curiosity or discovery. There was nothing contrary to her habits in taking an ante-meridian walk, whether to the village for a skein of wool or other such trifling errand, or simply for the sake of a stroll to the garden or in the meadows, where the foals were playing by their mothers' feet. Honor felt persuaded, therefore, that unless any chance observer, any officious gossip, after tracing her to the station, returned to spread through the village the intelligence of her flight, that all-important event would not, in all probability for several hours after, be discovered. The return of John Beacham to his dinner, which he was in the habit of doing, unless detained on business, punctually at four, would of course be the signal for a search after the missing woman; and Honor, as the hours wore on (and they passed very slowly after the inditing and taking to the nearest post of her second note to Arthur Vavasour), could scarcely keep her mind for many minutes together from wandering back again to home, and to the imagined scene of grief and consternation which the certainty of her flight would cause. She found herself for the first time in her life alone; alone, and left solely to her own resources, not only for the support of existence (that was to be an after and less important consideration), but left to provide her own thoughts, to steady her own nerves—the nerves on which a few short hours of loneliness were beginning to tell; left, in short, to what is so unnatural a condition for the young and feeble—left to be mistress of herself.

Two circumstances alone enabled Honor in that dreary upper chamber, smelling of the stale tobacco used by a very inferior class of "gentlemen lodgers," and displaying in its dingy furniture and generally shabby gentility unfailing evidences of wear and tear as well as of slovenly and uncleanly habits — two circumstances alone enabled Honor to bear with tolerable patience the

situation in which she had voluntarily plunged
herself. In the first place, so prone are we to
judge and draw our decisions from effects without seeking after causes, Honor still took a curious
kind of comfort from the conviction that she was,
in her humble way, a martyr and a victim. This
belief, which she hugged perseveringly to her
heart, was for a time a decided but gradually
lessening set-off against the *ennui* which, creeping gradually over her spirits, caused her to long
exceedingly for the second and more tangible
form of consolation—namely, the advent of the
only friend that in that vast metropolis she could
boast of possessing. The ideas of this young
woman from the country regarding the time requisite to convey a letter from one district to
another were somewhat vague and methodless;
and therefore it was that, long before the dainty
little epistle, which she trusted would bring
Arthur to her side, had (in all probability) been
taken from the pillar-box into which she had
thrown it, Honor had begun to hope that her
friend would ere long be by her side. In thus
hoping it never occurred to her that she was
acting wickedly. It was true that Arthur had,
at the commencement of their friendship, uttered
foolish words that had startled, if not angered
her; but she had given him to understand plainly,

though kindly, that such words were an offence and an annoyance, and since that he had never —no, *never*, Honor repeated to herself as the recollection of certain meaning glances and too tender pressings of her yielded hand crowded thick upon her, and gave the lie (deny the impeachment though she might) to her assertion—he had *never* once appeared to view her in any other light than as a valued friend. Of the birth of Arthur's little son, and of the semi-imprisonment to the house to which Mr. Vavasour had in consequence been condemned, Honor knew nothing. To her the fact of his being a father, one with such a title to respect and consideration as that name bestowed, would, had she been aware of the event that had occurred in Hyde-park-gardens, have probably checked her eagerness to make known her whereabouts to Arthur. She was one of those women by whom the possession of a child is looked upon as a very sacred thing— one of the many of her sex was she who are not and cannot be wholly and completely women till the ineffable joys, the pains, and pleasures of maternity, have set their stamp upon the youthful brow, and called forth the slumbering but best and deepest feelings of their nature.

Strange as it may seem, Honor's liking— friendship, call it what you will—was but another phase and form of mother's love.   Arthur was, or at least he said he was, unhappy; he was in debt and difficulty—possibly, too, in disgrace; surely these were reasons for the granting him the tender pity that is akin to love—the pity that every true and devoted mother feels for the helpless children of her affection.

Thinking of Arthur Vavasour—thinking of him alternately with her gradually-increasing sorrow for the husband she had deserted—Honor passed the hours wearily enough away, and it was something of a relief when, about five o'clock, Mrs. Casey, slightly improved in appearance by the afternoon's "cleaning," knocked at the door, and a good deal more familiarly than was altogether agreeable to Honor, inquired of that mysterious young person whether she didn't feel inclined to take anything.

"Only some tea," Honor said, "and soon, please."

She was beginning to feel rather faint from fasting, and the thought of tea and bread-and-butter, albeit the cates to be provided by Mrs. Casey were little likely to be tempting, was rather agreeable to her imagination.

"Directly," was the prompt reply of the woman whom Honor, though she could not have told the reason why, liked less well every time

she saw her. And Mrs. Casey was as good, and
indeed, to Honor's annoyance, even better than
her word; for with "the tea," which made its
appearance in the form of battered Britannia
metal, cracked and cemented crockery, damp
bread, and sky-blue milk, came in due form, and
with a manner that was decidedly patronising,
the landlady herself. Seating herself on the comfortless little sofa by Honor's side, the Widow
Casey (Honor might, if she had cared to listen,
have speedily known a good deal concerning that
respectable person's antecedents) commenced a
series of what *she* imagined to be highly ingenious and diplomatic queries regarding her lodger's
birth and parentage, her education and her antecedents. To the best of her ability, Honor
warded off the danger of making any direct reply to these troublesome investigations. She had
taken the precaution to remove her wedding-
ring, and could therefore pass herself off as Miss
Blake, an orphan whose friends were tired of
supporting her, and who was therefore desirous
of finding her own living in the best way she
could. The person she was expecting was a *married* gentleman. Honor laid especial stress on
that fact, though it was quite evident that Mrs.
Casey's " O, indeed !" did not proclaim any very
satisfactory effect produced upon *her* mind by the

knowledge of Mr. Vavasour's connubial condition. After that trifling episode, the self-invited visitor remained for a good hour, as if glued to the piece of furniture of which she had taken uninvited possession; and it was owing to no absence of loquacity on her part if, before that hour was over, Honor was not well aware of certain interesting portions of her landlady's family history—namely, that she too had the bad luck to be an "orphan;" that Casey, poor fellow, loved his drop, which was often a loss and a hindrance to *her* well-doing; that her favourite son had been drowned at sea, and her daughter had just five months before married a gentleman in the surveying line, who had his horse and shay, and could keep her, bless you! like a lady.

CHAPTER XVIII.

JOHN DISCOVERS HIS LOSS.

Four o'clock had long ago struck,—for those were busy times for John, and people who could not be put off came to him at all hours on matters connected with his *industrie*,—four o'clock had long ago struck before John's hearty voice—it was the kind of voice that sent a feeling of serenity through the whole house in which it had a right to resound—made itself heard in the hall and passages of Pear-tree House.

"Mother! Hallo! O, there you are." And then it was, "Where's Honor, mother? Upstairs, eh?"

Mrs. Beacham both looked and felt uncomfortable. It was now many hours since she had seen the daughter-in-law whose feelings she was well aware she had galled and wounded to the utmost. Where those hours had been spent by Honor—whether in the solitude of her own room, or wandering out into the fields—whether in paying a visit to her friends the Clays (at which news Mrs. Beacham would have secretly greatly rejoiced), the latter knew not. All of which she felt quite certain was, that John would demand a strict account of his wife's proceedings, whether those proceedings were voluntary or otherwise; and if Honor had in very truth been some seven or eight hours alone and without food, the old lady did not doubt that he would be very seriously displeased. John was not habitually an observant man; but there was that in his mother's face which made him suspect that something was wrong. That she had been, during his absence, harsh with, if not, indeed, positively unkind to, his young wife, was, however, the worst of John Beacham's fears; but these were disagreeable and annoying enough; and it was with the evident irritation of a hasty-tempered man that he repeated the words:

"Where is Honor? She isn't ill, mother, is she? Or" (more nervously still) "is anything the matter?"

"Nothing, that I know of," replied Mrs. Beacham ceremoniously. It always provoked her to see John "fussing," as she called it, over his wife. "Honor is in her own room, I suppose, looking over her finery, as usual. If you want her, you had better call her down."

John waited not to hear this piece of advice.

A strange but faint presentiment of evil—not the evil that *had* overtaken him, that was too terrible to have entered even the outside confines of his imagination, but a sense that some annoyance was preparing—oppressed and worried him. Mounting the stairs with hasty footsteps, and calling his wife's name the while, he was very speedily at the chamber-door, where he tapped—as was his wont —very softly for admittance,—softly at first; and then, receiving no reply, he repeated the summons more noisily; but still without the desired effect. Then, and not till then, he entered, and was surprised—though not yet roused to a state of alarm —by the condition in which he found the usually neat and well-ordered sleeping-room. On the bed, which, tossed and tumbled, bore marks of having been pressed by the weight of a reclining and very restless figure, lay near the pillow a handkerchief still wet with abundant tears; while open drawers, a small, very small, jewel-casket standing—not its usual place—conspicuously upon the toilet-table, and a certain general disarray suggestive of departure, made, for a single moment, John's heart to stand still within him for fear.

"Mother!" he cried, calling loudly from the top of the stairs, "for the love of God come here, and, if you can, tell me," he went on excitedly, and laying his hand heavily on the bannisters to steady himself (the old lady, after making what haste she could, stood beside him on the landing) —"tell me, if you can, what has become of Honor."

"What has become of her? Why, what makes you think that anything has become of her?" retorted his mother, endeavouring to hide her own alarm by ill-acted bluster. "Nothing ever becomes of anybody that I know of. What in goodness' name do you mean?"

But in spite of her attempts to carry off matters with a high hand, Mrs. Beacham's courage did begin to fail her at sight of the evidences of a sudden and desperate resolution with which, to her thinking, the room abounded. John, watching her countenance narrowly, drew his own auguries from what he read there.

"Mother," he said sternly, "may God forgive me if I am wrong, but I fear—I cannot help fearing—that you have something to do with—with what Honor—with what my poor wife may have done."

"I? What should I have to do with it?" she asked; but her voice trembled as she spoke, and sitting down hastily on the nearest chair, she waited in silence for what was to follow.

"I don't know—I can't tell; my head seems

in a whirl; but tell me—that at any rate you can do, mother—when did you see Honor last?"

"At about ten o'clock, or thereabouts. You had been gone about half an hour when she went upstairs."

"And have none of the servants seen her since?"

"I don't know; you had better ask. I daresay it will turn out that she is somewhere close by, —or gone to the Clays perhaps,—and that you have been making a great deal of fuss about nothing."

On this hint John at once acted. The idea that Honor might be paying a visit to her old friends was a possible, though scarcely a probable, solution of his difficulty; and he caught at it with eager hope. From the servants, when questioned, he could learn but little. Hannah had seen her young mistress with her hat on walking across the garden towards the village. She had not noticed whether Mrs. John had anything in her hand or not. She might have, *sure-ly*, for anything that Hannah knew. She didn't take much heed, not she, being busy at the time, and thinking the missus was only going for a walk like.

"Which I daresay she was," John said more hopefully; "and, mother, if you'll go to your dinner—I am very sorry I kept you so long waiting —I'll look about a bit for Honor; and if it happens that I don't find her, why I'll ride over to the Clays and bring her back."

Acting on this resolution,—for it was a matter of *necessity* to search actively for Honor, since sitting down quietly under his suspense would drive him mad he thought,—John hurried away down the sweet-brier hedge that ran at right-angles with the porch—hurried away so quickly that his mother had no time to reiterate her urgent entreaty that he would have something to eat before he went.

" Just a mouthful, John!" she screamed at the very top of her voice, as she caught a last glimpse of his tall figure turning an angle in the path.

But her anxiety was entirely thrown away. A shake of the head was all the answer that John vouchsafed; for the miserably anxious man, whose appetite for his dinner was usually of the healthiest and keenest, felt at that moment that he should not care either to eat or sleep again till he had found the wife that he had lost.

CHAPTER XIX.

ANOTHER ESCAPE.

"A gentleman, please, miss, as wants to see you."

Such was the announcement, on the morning succeeding Honor's instalment in her new abode, of the fastidious Arthur Vavasour's visit to that very untempting "bower of beauty."

In was nearly noon, an early hour for *him* to be abroad; but to Honor—who had passed a sleepless night, and who had been up and about for ages, as it seemed to her—the day appeared to be already well-nigh spent; while as regarded him, and her chance of seeing him in her wretched home, she had begun almost to despair of any such blissful, and now apparently improbable, event. When he *did* appear therefore, when her hand was clasped in his, and when his kind voice whispered softly, "I could not come before, dear; and now I *am* come, what a place

I find you in!" her heart went forth with grateful joy to meet him, for she felt no longer unprotected and alone.

"And so they have been ill-using you, you poor little thing?" he went on softly, her hand still in his, as they sat side by side on what Mrs. Casey called the couch. "I guessed how it would be; I did not like the way he looked when he took you away that night."

"O, but it isn't John—*indeed* it isn't!" Honor said eagerly, her sense of justice roused to defend her husband; "it was his mother, as I told you, who behaved so to me. It was she that made me go. I know it was wrong; but what could I do?"

"What indeed?" stroking tenderly the little hand he held in his. "But, Honor, it will never do for you to remain here. The place is not respectable—I am certain it is not; and the woman looks like an ogress. I think I can manage something better for you than this. There is an old servant of my father's—a Swiss—an excellent man, with one of the cleanest and most cheerful of little wives; and if he happens to have room in his house, I am sure he will be only too delighted to devote himself to making you comfortable. Really, the nicest of old men. I will go there this afternoon, and try to make arrangements for the change."

"Thank you—how good you are!" Honor said fervently; "they certainly do not seem like nice people here; but I stopped at the first place where I saw a bill up. I believe I was afraid to meet my father. What I fear most now is his seeing me; for he would perhaps tell John—John would go to him first, you know, and—"

"Your father! Why, Honor, haven't you heard? But I don't know how you should. Your father is—has—" and then he stopped, feeling it scarcely decent to disclose to Honor the facts that proclaimed her father to be a villain.

But his companion, who was *quoad* curiosity a true daughter of Eve, refused on this occasion to allow her filial feelings to be spared. She insisted (and as a natural consequence not only of that insistence, but of the wronged man's easily-to-be-comprehended satisfaction in giving at least words to his sorrow) on hearing all that Arthur could tell her of her father. In breathless silence she listened to a detail of his villany; and deep indeed and painful was her regret at the injury which had been done to the man who had so blindly trusted him.

As Arthur noted the quivering lip, the turbulent heaving of the pitying breast, he could not but feel he was in one respect a gainer by his loss; for Honor *could* hardly be hard and distant to the friend who had fallen a victim to the machinations of her father. Arthur felt that he had claim on, an actual right to, her sympathy and kindness now, and therefore did not hesitate to make the very most of the injuries, the losses, and the embarrassments which the Colonel's baseness had entailed upon him.

"I am *so* sorry—so very grieved. Is there nothing that I could do? Perhaps if I were to see my father, I might—"

Arthur interrupted her with a laugh. "See him?" he said; "why, it would require the best detective in London, I suspect, to find him out; and if we did, there is nothing, not even *your* persuasions, which would be likely to work up such a man as Fred Norcott to his duty. But we have wasted time enough over him, dear Honor; and as I am not my own master just now—since Sophy's confinement, I mean—"

"Since *that*? O, Mr. Vavasour, why *did* you not tell me before? You knew I should care so much to hear it! Think of your having a dear little child!" and she sighed involuntarily, a faint but very mournful sigh (which Arthur fancied in his folly that he comprehended), and then added, with an attempt at playfulness, "Perhaps I may be thought clever enough to teach your children some day; but I must learn a great deal myself first. The Miss Vavasours will want all sorts of accomplishments that a humble nursery governess knows nothing about; and that reminds me—" speaking very quick, as she noted a crimson flush that mounted to her companion's brow, and a something in his eyes which her woman's instinct taught her was alarming—" that reminds me that I have no time to lose in looking for the means of providing for myself. I have a good deal of money" (there were exactly seven pounds in her portemonnaie), "but still I want to begin. It will be no trouble to me to teach and take care of children. I love them so dearly; and the little things always take to me."

"It would be strange, I think, if they did not," Arthur ventured to say, as he gazed with such passionate fondness on her face, that Honor was forced to veil her eyes with their white lids for very shame.

"O no, it isn't that," she said hastily, and hardly knowing what words were falling from her lips. "You see, I have been so used to them, and—and I cannot bear to be idle. If I have nothing to do, I begin to think—to think of poor John—"

Arthur, at this unexpected mention (a very

mal à propos one in his opinion) of an absent husband's name, rose abruptly from his place by Honor's side. He was very young, very little conversant in the ways and means of defence of such women as Honor, or he would have seen through this simple *ruse*. He would have understood that this beautiful and defenceless creature, with an instinctive dread of her pursuer, had thrown up this rampart against attack, and would have drawn, through that very alarm, good augury for eventual success.

It was fortunate for Honor that no such ideas as these entered at that moment the mind of the man who was gradually coming near enough to be—there is no medium course, let women believe in its existence if they will—either accepted or denied. It was well, too, that Arthur, roused by his own movement from the dream of passion in which he had been indulging, once more began to have some thought and memory for outward things, and especially for the lapse of time since he had left his home.

Looking hastily at his watch, he perceived to his dismay that it was four o'clock, so swiftly had time passed—is it not ever so?—while he had been occupied by talking about himself, and been busied with his own sentimental interests.

" Four o'clock already !" he exclaimed, " and

I have so much to do for you, Honor! It is impossible for you to remain here. I could not answer for the consequences. I only wish that I had met you at the Waterloo station, and prevented your coming here at all. However, I am off now to see about old Schmidt, and directly I have settled anything, I will return. In the mean time, do not leave the house, and if you can, avoid seeing the woman that it belongs to."

"I can hardly help seeing her," Honor said with a smile; for she was both amused and flattered by his solicitude on her behalf. "She *will* bring in the few things that I want herself, and—"

"Your poor little dinner solitary among the rest, I suppose?" said Arthur pityingly. "O Honor!" he continued—and how at that moment he longed for the hundredth time to take her in his arms and whisper to her his love, the object of that love was happily never destined to know—"O Honor!" he said, "my love, my darling! how unfitted you are to do battle for yourself in this rough, wicked world! It is so hard to leave you, so hard to think of you, in this sordid miserable place, alone, unprotected, and—God help both you and me!—so very, very beautiful!"

He drew a long, almost a gasping breath, as the last passionate words burst from his white quivering lips, and, almost before Honor could even look her surprise at the utterly unexpected outburst, the door had closed upon his retreating figure, and Honor once more found herself alone.

CHAPTER XX.

POOR SOPHY !

"I AM so glad they have let me see you, though I *am* only to speak in a whisper, and to stay just one half-hour and no more. You darling thing! How pretty you look in that dear little cap!" And Katie Vavasour, who had been allowed, as a great favour, to visit her much-loved sister-in-law, pressed her fresh young lips to the invalid's forehead, and took her seat beside the bed preparatory to a "quiet talk."

"I am glad you came too, dear," Sophy rejoined. "It is so dull without Arthur, and he has been gone away so long—many hours, I am sure. What o'clock is it now? Three, I am sure; and he left me long before twelve. Where do you think he is?"

"O, I don't know. Gone somewhere about horses, I daresay," rejoined Kate, who was rather glad of Arthur's absence, since it enabled her to have Sophy to herself. "But tell me, does he love the baby *very* much? Does he often kiss it?"

"No, not often; indeed, I don't think he ever has; but I shouldn't mind that, if he would but come back," said poor Sophy, whose nerves were weak (a malady which her young sister-in-law found it hard to understand), and whose impatience at her husband's absence was often a little trying to those about her.

"O, never mind him. There is no use ever in wondering what men are about," said unsympathising Kate. "I want to tell you about poor Rhoda. I am certain she is pining for that stupid Mr. Wallingford. It would not have been a nice match, of course; but as she liked him, that ought to be enough; and Rhoda was never strong, and now she looks like a ghost."

"Poor thing!" murmured Sophy. "But if I remember right, Mr. Wallingford had straight hair and a long neck, and seemed terribly *poky.*"

"Exactly; but if Rhoda did not think so, what did it signify?" was Kate's somewhat involved rejoinder. "All I know is, that if anything bad happens, it will be mamma's fault. O, she is so dreadfully hard and proud and unfeeling! And she will be worse than ever, if she gets the better of poor Arthur about the property. O, Sophy! is it not too bad that she should have things all

her own way like this? Do you know, I would
give ten years of my life—"

"To be taken in your old age, of course," put
in Sophy, with something of her former girlish
playfulness.

"O, yes; that of course," said Kate; "and
besides—"

But the current of her confidences was at that
moment checked by the entrance through the adjoining boudoir of Mrs. Vavasour's maid, who, in
a hesitating voice, made the whispered announcement that a person calling himself Mr. Beacham
was below, and was very anxious to have speech
with one of the family. Both Mr. Duberly and
Mr. Vavasour were out of the way, the woman
said, so she had thought it best to come to Miss
Catherine about it.

"I will go down directly," Kate said; but of
this, Sophy, with the caprice common to invalids,
would not hear. She insisted, for some reason
best known to herself, on Mr. Beacham being
shown into the boudoir.

"You can see him there, dear," she said to
Kate; "he is a sort of gentleman you know"
(poor, *poor* John!); "and I shall not be left alone,
which I hate."

Foreseeing no reason for objecting to her sister-in-law's wish, Kate gave the necessary direc-

tions, and in a few more moments a man's strong, vigorous step was heard treading the Aubusson carpet in Sophy's " morning-room."

" I beg your pardon, Miss Vavasour," John said aloud—he was totally ignorant of the fact that within earshot lay the sick and nervous wife of the man he had come to seek, the man against whom he felt as an enemy so bitter that blood could neither wash out the offence, nor quench the rage that burnt so madly in his veins—" I beg your pardon, but I require to know if you will have the goodness to tell me where I am likely to find your brother, Mr. Arthur Vavasour. The people down below, the servants, seem too grand to answer questions, so I am driven to the masters for information. He is not, I suppose, in the house, hiding behind his wife's apron-string? He—"

" Hush! For Heaven's sake speak lower," said Kate in an eager whisper. It was so dreadful to think that Sophy *might* hear, although the rooms were large and there was no great probability of such a catastrophe, but still the sound of John's angry words *might* reach the ears of Arthur's wife; and Kate, girl though she was, could foresee and dread the consequences of such a terrible calamity. " Speak lower," she said a little proudly, for there was a spice of her mother's *hauteur* in her veins, and Kate Vavasour chafed under the familiar *brusquerie* of one beneath her.

"Speak lower, do you say? And why? Is this man, this base betrayer of—but I beg your pardon once more. You are a young lady, Miss Vavasour; one of a class that is protected from insult and wrong by the shield of position and a great name. A name, forsooth! Why *mine* was, in its humble way, respected once; respected till your brother came—your brother, whose father was my friend—and dragged the honour of my house, *my* honour—" and he dealt a savage blow on his broad breast—"in the dust! My wife has left me," he groaned out; "*that* can be no secret now—left me for him, although I never knew it was so till to-day. It was yesterday I lost her; lost the poor child I loved so well: and in the evening I inquired for her at her rascal father's house, but they could, or perhaps would not tell me anything. But to-day I went again, and forced them to be more explicit. Then I learnt how *he* had, while she was with her father, how he had spent his days, his evenings, all his time, with Honor. I came here three hours ago, and tried to learn something of the man's movements—something which would guide me to my wife; but all the answer was that he had been out for hours, no one could tell me where; but the rascal that I spoke to grinned, and hinted of a lady's letter till I was almost driven mad; and here I am, hoping that you, at least, will not—"

He was interrupted by a cry—a cry, feeble it is true, but so piercing and peculiar in its tone that it haunted his brain afterwards for weeks; then there was the sound of a heavy fall—a fall which Kate knew, in the twinkling of an eye, was that of poor Sophy's lifeless body on the floor. In a moment all was wild confusion; a very Babel of cries and consternation; and John Beacham (awakened, when too late, to a sense of the evil which his intemperate words had wrought) lifted the inanimate form of the poor young wife in his strong arms, and laid her gently on the bed from which a fatal curiosity had roused her. Verily in the old tale of Bluebeard there is much and truthful knowledge of female nature, for to every woman there is a subtle and terrible attraction in the *bloody key;* and to know that which it is well for their peace that they should ignore, has ever been an insatiable craving amongst the fair daughters of Eve.

Poor Kate proved herself fully equal to the emergency in which she found herself. Forgetful of John Beacham's hasty and passionate revelations, she could only think of him in the light of an able-bodied man, ready and willing to do good service to the helpless.

"Try and find her father," she said imploringly; while the monthly nurse, who had already despatched a messenger for the physician in attendance, was endeavouring, with no apparent result, to restore animation to poor Sophy's apparently lifeless body. "Try and find Mr. Duberly. Perhaps he will be at the Union Club; and Arthur, poor Arthur! *he* ought to be here. Mr. Beacham," she continued with imploring eagerness, the thought of her brother bringing back the memory of the man's desperate words, "Mr. Beacham, at such a moment you cannot, will not, think of yourself. You see what your words have done. Poor, poor Sophy!" And the tears fell in torrents from her blinded eyes. "You will find Arthur for *her*. I do not believe in his wickedness. He may have been foolish, but he loved his wife and little child; you have been deceived; and it is all a dreadful, dreadful mistake."

John shook his head gloomily. He was too convinced of his former friend's share in his wife's flight for any words to alter his convictions. Men who are habitually unsuspicious are often the most tenacious of a dark idea when once it has taken root within their breasts; and John's present belief was, he then felt assured, for *life*. But cer-

tain although he was of Arthur Vavasour's guilt,
he could not view, without the bitterest remorse,
the wreck that his untamed passion had wrought
in that so lately happy and prosperous home.
There was no need now for Kate to press upon
him the duty of forbearance. God, the Judge of
sinners, had taken the task of retribution into His
own hands; for if it were indeed true, as Miss
Vavasour had asserted, that Arthur loved his wife,
why, in that pale corse lying lifeless before him,
his own wrongs, the wrongs inflicted by the bereaved husband, would indeed be fearfully and
terribly avenged. Well he knew that to himself,
as the acting cause of that dire catastrophe, poor
Sophy's death (if, as seemed only too probable,
her pale head was never to be raised in life again)
might be traced; and it was with his already
heavily-burdened spirit weighted with another
load, that John Beacham, with the purpose of
fulfilling Kate Vavasour's behest, and endeavouring to seek out poor Sophy's father, prepared to
leave the house where his presence had been pro-
ductive of results as unexpected as they were de-
plorable. But he was not destined to go many
steps before a fresh call was made upon his patience and his temper. On the threshold of that
splendid mansion, drawing forth the latch-key
with which he had just opened the door, there

stood, confronting the departing visitor, no less important a personage than Arthur Vavasour himself. On seeing John, he started visibly and turned pale—not with the pallor of fear, for at that instant very thankful was the younger man that he had no serious wrongs, as regarded his father's friend, with which to reproach himself; but the sight of John Beacham perplexed and startled him. It was connected, of course, with Honor's flight from home; and there existed, undoubtedly, a certain awkwardness in the fact that he, Arthur, was so much better informed regarding Honor's whereabouts than was the husband from whom that misguided young woman ought, in the opinion of sticklers for marital rights, have had no secrets of any kind whatsoever.

" *You* here ! Beacham, how is this?" Arthur said, holding out a hand which was not taken; and then the anger of the older man, a moment controlled by the sight he had just witnessed abovestairs, burst out afresh. Drawing Arthur Vavasour's slender form back into the house, and holding the arm of his enemy with the fixedness of a vice, he said in a voice tremulous with concentrated passion,

" You ask me, do you, why I am here ? What if, in return, I call you *scoundrel,* and ask you where you have taken my wife? for you have

been with her; I see it in your face—your white,
cowardly face. God, that I should live to speak
so to your father's son!" And, half-overpowered
with contending emotions, John sank upon a chair
that stood in the large empty hall, and gazed for
a moment helplessly upon the young handsome
features, which at that terrible moment reminded
him strangely of Cecil Vavasour, of the man whom
in all his life he had most loved and respected.

"John," Arthur exclaimed, "do not, for God's
sake, talk in this way. I declare before Heaven
that you are mistaken. I swear to you that your
wife—"

"Have you seen her? Do you know where
she is?" cried John impetuously. Poor fellow! he
would have caught only too gladly at the belief
that his suspicions were unfounded, and that his
still dearly loved Honor had been foolish only, but
not guilty. O no, not guilty! the thought of that
evil was too dreadful to be endured; so he said
very eagerly, and with a touching entreaty in his
tone, "Mr. Vavasour, only say—swear it to me
by your father's memory—that within these three
days you have neither seen nor heard from my
wife, and I will thank and bless you to my dying
day."

But Arthur could not, dared not, swear to
this. With all his longing, not only to save

Honor, but to console and reassure the excellent man who had ever treated him with such frank and cordial kindness, he could not take the oath required of him. He could not, even for the woman whom he loved, *quite* drag what he called his honour in the dirt.

The sight of his hesitation was enough, and more than enough, to confirm the husband's worst apprehensions; and to what lengths his passion would have carried him, had not this stormy interview been interrupted, it would be hard to say. Already John had begun to pour a torrent of invectives on the young man's head, when the sight of Kate Vavasour running, almost flying, down the broad marble staircase, arrested his words.

"Arthur, Arthur!" she screamed, "for the love of Heaven, for poor Sophy's sake, come away. She is dying—dead, they think," she added distractedly, for, in very truth, she scarcely knew what she said; "and *you have killed her!*"

CHAPTER XXI

ALAS, alas for the young creature that was taken, and for the old man that was left behind! Kate's words were only too true; and Sophy, the loved of many hearts—the wealthy heiress, on whose bright blooming face the winds of heaven had never been allowed to play too roughly—was numbered with the dead. She never spoke again, after they laid her upon her bed by the side of her sleeping infant; and that she died unconscious of the truth—that the frantic denials poured forth in his agony by Arthur of the guilt and treachery of which he had been accused, fell upon ears that heard them not—was, perhaps, the bitterest portion of his punishment. That he had been accused unjustly, and that he had in reality never what is called *wronged* the tender wife who had paid for her jealous curiosity with her life, was Arthur's only consolation in his hour of trial and bereavement. He forgot that his freedom from actual guilt was owing to no virtue on his own part; forgot that in his heart he had committed the sin the bare accusation of which, overheard by his poor Sophy, had consigned her to an early grave; forgot that while *she* was tender, loving, and true, his heart, ever since he had led her to the altar, had been bound up in, and wholly occupied by, another. But if, in his yearning for self-comfort, and in the natural longing of cowardly mortals to escape from the sharp stings of conscience, Arthur Vavasour could find consolation in the reflection that he had escaped *actual* guilt, there was one who, from the hour when he was first prostrated to the earth by the intelligence of poor Sophy's death to the day when his own sorrows were buried in the grave, could never bring himself to see any mitigation of Arthur Vavasour's offence, or any plea for mercy on the ground that he had not been, in *fact*, faithless to his marriage-vows. To describe the grief, the frantic despair it might rather be called, of the father whose only child was thus, in the bloom of her innocent and happy youth, torn from his arms and from his love, would be impossible. The blow had, indeed, fallen with terrible suddenness on the aged head that never, never again rose erect, as it had done before, with the proud, glad look that prosperity and domestic content are wont to lend to their possessors. "Old Dub" (there was such a touching solemnity, a sacredness as it were, thrown around his undying grief, that the name seemed no longer to suit him, and died away speedily, as do the nicknames of children when age and wisdom renders their foolish *petits noms* inappropriate and absurd), "old Dub" was never the same man again after he had seen the delicate limbs of his dead daughter laid out for her burial. It was a touching sight to witness, that of the gray hairs falling over the white closed eyelids of the corpse, while the scant tears of age wrung from a father's agony fell slowly one by one upon poor Sophy's marble forehead. At the foot of the bed Arthur, pale almost as the dead that lay in its dread immovability before him, stood with folded arms, and with ever and anon a strong shiver shaking him from head to foot. He felt (it is the nature of his sex and kind) a good deal for himself, even in those moments of deep grief and self-reproach; and certain questions *would* intrude themselves on his mind which were out of place in the breast of a newly-made widower, and in the chamber of mourning. Would Mr. Duberly, who knew nothing at present of the share which he (Arthur) had in poor Sophy's death,— would he be *very* hard upon him if, which was only too probable, he should come to know the

truth? Would he believe in Arthur's assurances,
on his oath, that John Beacham's visit had been
the act of a madman, an act unjustified by any
conduct, any intentions on Arthur's part to injure
or to wrong him? That the old man, sorrowing
with a grief which would not be comforted, and
lamenting over his lost treasure with " groanings
that could not be uttered," would not so believe,
Arthur more than suspected. Well did he remember the jealous watchfulness, the unceasing
solicitude, with which this doting father had striven
to guard his child from even a transient sorrow;
and it was not difficult to imagine the fury that
would rage within his breast when the truth should
be revealed to him that Arthur was, as Kate Vavasour had in her agony of fear and love exclaimed, his daughter's murderer !

Meanwhile, these two were not alone in enduring, with such patience as in the first dark
moments of bereavement we can summon to our
aid, the consequences of guilty passions, of deceit, of vanity, and of folly. Watching, waiting,
grieving,—watching and waiting for the friend
who came not, and grieving with bitter tears over
her past folly,—Honor sat in the dismal chamber
of that dirty and barely respectable lodging-house
—a piteous sight, indeed, to look upon. As usual,
the sense of error had been the result of mortifica-

tion and of sorrow. *Le remord est né de l'abandon et non pas de la faute;* and if Arthur Vavasour had not been prevented in a manner as yet un-dreamt-of by Honor from keeping his engagement with her, and aiding her in the course which she had faintly marked out for herself, it is probable that Honor would have been far longer than was actually the case in arriving at a due and contrite sense of her *mistakes.* The hours after Arthur's departure dragged on very wearily for the imprudent girl who, a prisoner in that dis-mal room, began, as the time wore on and she heard nothing either of or from him, very seri-ously and repentantly to commune with her own thoughts. It was then that the mist of prejudice in favour of a class above her cleared away for ever; then that she no longer craved to be what is conventionally termed a "lady;" then that she learned (the teaching was a severe and un-compromising one, but none the less effectual be-cause of the heavy hand that had been raised in teaching her)—then it was that she learned the valuable truth that sterling worth is more to be desired than the outside graces of a soft manner and a flattering tongue, and that the heart of gold is better than the glitter of a refined and fair ap-pearance. Instead of inwardly glorying in her near kindred to the well-born, and in lieu of re-

joicing over the fact that *she* came of a gentle race,
and that in her veins ran the pure Norman blood
of the well-descended "Norcotts of Archerfield,"
Honor Beacham would henceforth shrink in shame
from the memory of her parentage, bearing ever
before her the unwelcome and dishonouring truth,
that the man to whom she owed the birth on which
she had been weak enough to pride herself was, in
very truth, nothing better than a swindler!

And out of the painful conviction that so it
was there grew another, and if possible a still
more harrowing thought—the thought, namely,
of the more than possibility which existed of a life-
long separation (the consequence of her own impatience under what appeared to her now chastened
spirit in the light of very minor grievances) from
the husband whose excellence she was tardily beginning to value as it deserved. It was true that
she had committed no act which must of necessity
cause an eternal breach between them, and equally
true was it that she had, previous to her departure,
written a half-protesting, half-apologetic letter—
the letter of which the reader is already cognisant,
and which (on such apparently trifling causes do
the most important events of our lives depend)
was not delivered at Pear-tree House till *after* its
owner's fatal visit to London—it was true, I repeat, that Honor had written a letter which *might*,

she felt, eventually soften John's heart towards
her. In it she had explained, as well as she was
able—she could not abuse as heartily as she wished
John's mother to John himself—but in it she had
not disguised the fact that the old lady's unkindness was the sole motive cause of her departure;
nor had she hesitated to assure the husband she
was leaving that she might, under other circumstances, have lived happily beneath his roof.

How keenly, as Honor strove to call to mind
the only half-remembered expressions in that
hastily-written epistle, did she regret that she
had not endeavoured to fix them more firmly
on her memory; for every syllable that she had
written seemed to her of importance now, when
wondering to herself what John was thinking of
her, and whether or not she was beyond the reach
of pardon.

Of Mrs. Beacham she had not yet brought
herself to think with charity. If the possibility
of a return to the Paddocks lingered for a moment
in her mind, that possibility was rendered so dark
and unattractive by the image of her mother-in-
law, that Honor, although beginning to long for
reconciliation with John, turned from it with as
much detestation as it was in her gentle and affectionate nature to feel. Not yet was she thoroughly
and effectually subdued; not yet had the chasten-

ing rod of affliction done its perfect work. Honor
still found herself, when the *good* spirit within was
drawing her to an *entire* oblivion of her wrongs—
to a perfect pardon of the past, and to a self-effacing
sense of her own unworthiness—she still, I say, in
spite of her sometimes conviction that she ought,
in deep humility, to entreat forgiveness of her
aged persecutor, shrunk with very natural repug-
nance from such an act of self-abasement. The
provocations she had received *would* rise up in
her memory, like evil ghosts that refused to be
laid to rest; while it was as yet, I fear, only in
theory that Honor regarded the endurance of
wrong with patience, as one of the first of Christian virtues. The time, however, came when she
not only believed, but demonstrated her faith by
practice, that the great duty of bearing and for-
bearing may be so gracefully, as well as rigidly
practised, that the fruits of such forbearance can
scarcely fail to be those of mutual affection, confidence, and good-will.

The obtrusive and constant visits of Mrs. Casey
did not tend to render poor Honor better satisfied
with her condition. That quick-sighted and not
over-charitable personage had drawn her own conclusions from the lengthened stay of a young and
handsome gentleman in the "second-floor front,"
and those conclusions had not tended to increase

her show of respect for the young lady—the "Miss Blake" who was so beautiful and *so be-friended.*

When the long day was at last over, and all chance of seeing Arthur till the following morning was at an end, Honor prepared herself for bed, with the heaviest heart for company she had ever known. With the impatience of suspense so common at her age, she asked herself how it was possible to wear through the hours till morning—the long and lonely hours in which she had naught to do save to turn and twist, and twist and turn again, the arguments for and against each possible reason for Arthur's breach of faith—the miserable hours during which she would be for ever saying with the sleepless victim of unrest recorded in Holy Writ: "Would God it were light! Would God it were the morning!"

But when morning came it brought with it no comfort for the lonely watcher. The hope which she had nourished that the early post would bring to her some explanation of the absence of her only friend proved a fruitless one; for though the sharp tap-tap of the postman's summons sounded clear and loud at the door of No. 29, there was no letter, so the little dirty drab of a servant-girl informed Honor, for *her;* and again the unhappy and restless creature, seated before her untempting and scarcely-tasted breakfast, was forced to summon all her fortitude to endure the scarcely endurable torments of uncertainty.

CHAPTER XXII

JOHN GIVES WAY.

WHEN John Beacham, after his worse than fruitless search after his missing wife, returned, which he at once did, to the Paddocks, Mrs. Beacham, though by no means addicted to sudden alarms, was startled by the change which a few short hours had wrought in his outer man. The soft spring evening was beginning to draw in, and the scent of the honeysuckle was filling the air, when the old lady, catching the sound of horse's hoofs (Tom Simmons's thoughtful care for the master whom he loved had prompted him to have Black Jenny in waiting at Switcham for the chance of John's return), laid down the knitting which was her unfailing occupation after dark, and stood beneath the blossoming woodbine that Honor loved, waiting to greet her son. He rode forward very slowly — so slowly that Mrs. Beacham, who had been accustomed for years to the brisk walk, verging on a trot, at which the

best rider in Sandyshire was in the habit of
bringing in his horse, imagined for a moment
that it could not be really John who came at
such a lingering, lagging pace towards his home.
But if the mother, who knew his ways so well,
thought that the step of her son, or rather that
of his good black steed, was strangely altered,
how much greater was the shock of surprise when,
by the failing light, she looked upon John's care-
worn face!

Throwing himself in a listless fashion, widely
different from his accustomed energetic movements, from the saddle, he stood by the old woman's side beneath the rustic porch, she looking
up with sad inquiry (for the suspense and worry
of the last six-and-thirty hours had quelled her
spirit) into her son's dulled and altered eyes.

"O, John!" she said pitifully, "dear, dear
John!" and then turning her head aside, for the
strong-minded old woman scorned her own weakness, she in secret wiped away the tears which
the sight of poor John's misery had wrung from
her aged eyes.

He put her very gently aside, so gently that
none could see the action, and then striding in
with a firm step to his own business-room, he
closed and locked the door. Truly he was in no
mood either to endure pity or submit to the ques-

tionings even of the mother who bore him. The return to his home, to the sight of familiar faces gazing at him with the compassion which was so hard to bear, had been in itself a severe trial to the proud man, to whom a good name was a treasure beyond price, and who could never —never, as he repeated with a terrible monotony to himself—hold up his head again. But grievous as these trials were, there was worse, much worse remaining behind; for the death of that poor young woman, who had so short a time before been full of life and happiness, lay (indirectly, it is true, but still it *did* lie—John never deceived himself on that point) on his own miserable head; and the weight of that death and the dread of it pursued him as might the swift footsteps of an avenging spirit, even into the stillness of his closet. Turn which way he would, all seemed dark around him. Alone henceforth, and while life should last (for since the evident impossibility on Arthur Vavasour's part to deny that he had seen Honor in London, the last ray of hope as regarded her virtue had been swept away)—alone in his deserted home—alone with his shame and his disgrace—what wonder was it that John Beacham, in the silence and solitude of his chamber, should have given way to a despondency that was twin-brother to despair?

A tap at the door, not a delicate or gentle one, for there were no genteel and well-trained servants at the Paddocks, roused the master of the house from the kind of stupor of grief into which he had fallen.

"A letter, please, sir," said a voice outside— the voice of Hannah, who, not finding her summons for admittance, promptly answered, had "tried the door," and *that* method of ingress having proved an unsuccessful one, she, with laudable perseverance, had hit upon another plan for the attainment of her object.

"A letter, please, sir," and, in a lower voice at the key-hole, "I think it is from the young missus."

The words, as Hannah had anticipated, acted like a charm. In a moment the door flew open under John's eager hand, and seizing the letter (it was the one which Honor had written previous to her departure, and which had remained ever since its delivery under Hannah's watchful care), he speedily succeeded, though the daylight was waning fast, in making himself master of its contents.

As he read the simple words—very simple they were, and childish, but each one carrying with it a proof of the writer's innocence and truth —the light of hope dawned once more on poor

John's darkened brain, and big tears of gratitude broke from his wearied eyes. Surprised, worn out both physically and mentally, for he had been more than thirty hours without rest or food, he could at first scarcely bring himself to understand the relief which, nevertheless, he felt was a great and blessed one. Laying his head down on his folded arms, with one short but fervent ejaculation of thankfulness hovering on his parched lips, the man whose iron frame had hitherto seemed almost impervious to fatigue, and proof against the ordinary ills that flesh is heir to, grew gradually insensible to outer things, losing all sense whether of joy or sorrow, in the heavy and lethargic slumber which is too often the precursor of serious illness.

Once and again, treading softly and on tiptoe, the old woman, anxious and miserable, stole to the side of the motionless figure, wondering at this unnatural quiet. But Hannah bade her not to worry herself.

"It's just nothing but being fairly worn out," she said, "and who's to wonder, I should like to know?" she went on defiantly. "A man, if he's as strong as Samson, can't abear being worritted for ever. Any way," the worthy creature said to herself, "I'm glad I kept the letter, maybe missus would have nobbled it; so she might.

There's never no knowing what some folks is up
to ;" and Hannah chuckled inwardly, as she set the
tea-things in preparation for the master's waking.

But neither on that occasion, nor for many a
day afterwards, did " the master," who was so
beloved by all who knew him, join in the daily
meals, the regular partaking of which those who
lead a simple life in farmhouses are wont to consider as absolutely necessary for the sustainment
of the vital principle existing within the human
frame. John awoke from the death-like slumber
into which he had fallen with shivering limbs
and an aching head; symptoms which even Mrs.
Beacham's limited experience told her denoted
the commencement of a violent fever; and such in
fact it proved. For many days John's life was in
serious danger; in such danger that the country
folk, coming from miles around to learn news of his
condition, lingered about for hours near the door,
expecting—fearing to hear the worst. In such
danger, that the poor old woman, his mother, knew
no rest either by night or day, for at the pillow
on which the fevered head lay tossing restlessly,
she listened remorsefully to his delirious ravings,
ravings in which were mingled in strange confusion the names of his lost Honor and of Arthur's
"murdered" wife.

CHAPTER XXIII.

HONOR RECEIVES A LETTER.

In the mean while Honor, unconscious of the events that had occurred, and the calamities which had befallen those in whom she was so deeply interested, had supported for another weary night and day the suspense which she found hourly more difficult of endurance. Then the courage that had hitherto supported her began to flag, and she half resolved — wholly objectionable as was the plan, and revolting to every feeling of womanly modesty—to endeavour by inquiry at Arthur's house to obtain some information concerning him. That some evil, some sudden accident or grievous sickness, had overtaken her only friend, Honor could not but believe; and it was this belief, joined to a certain pride which lingered in her still (for, after all, Arthur *might* be simply false), that prevented her from having recourse to her former plan—namely, that of writing to Arthur at his house or at his club. To sally

forth after dark; to call a cab, and to be driven
to within a few yards of Mr. Duberly's house;
and when there to make a few insignificant inquiries of the servant which might lead to something like elucidation of her doubts and fears,
seemed a plan not very difficult of execution; and
Honor was still pondering on its expediency when
to her surprise (for she had ceased to expect such
consolations) a letter was put into her hand by
Mrs. Casey—a letter, too, which she perceived at
once was from Arthur Vavasour.

Hurrying with her treasure into the inner
room, which was her bedchamber, and utterly re-
gardless of Mrs. Casey's feelings as a friend and
would-be confidante, Honor tore open the envelope, when the first writing that met her eye was
her own! Casting the note directed by herself
impatiently on one side, she opened another in-
closure—one of deeply-bordered mourning-paper,
and read as follows:

"MY DEAR HONOR,—For for the last time
I may venture to call you so; I write you this
letter to bid you a last farewell. A heavy blow
has fallen on us all. My poor wife—I did love
her, Honor, more than I ever thought—is dead. It
was very sudden. She overheard words—I trust
you may never know from whom—which must

have made her think that I was false to her, for
she fell down as one dead, poor girl, and never
spoke again. All this grief and wretchedness,
and the sight of poor Mr. Duberly's misery,
and knowing he must hate me soon, is more than
I can bear, so I have resolved that after the
funeral is over I will have an explanation — I
mean, that I will confess everything—about the
horse and my debts, and all my horrible decep-
tions to the poor old man; and after that, it is
my intention to go abroad, to America or some
distant country; and my best hope is that nobody
will ever hear of me again. Writing, as I am,
with the poor thing that I have killed so near
me, there are but few words, Honor, that I can
dare to say to you. One wish, one prayer, however, I *may* breathe, and that prayer is, that you
will go home to John. It is with the hope that
you will do so, that I send you back your own
innocent, simple notes, the only ones you ever
wrote to me, and which, but for the help that
they may be to you, I would never, *never* have
parted with. Send them to your husband, dear
Honor. They will convince him, if he is ever so
positive, that I was not a liar when I swore that
you were pure as the angels of Heaven from the
guilt of which he dared suspect you. And now,
dear Honor, fare you well, and if in the days to

come, when you are happy, as I pray you may
be, you should ever think of these past wretched
times again, let there be forgiveness in your heart
for one whose crime towards you has been followed by a punishment almost too heavy to be
borne."

Twice did Honor Beacham, with eyes blinded
by tears, read over this miserable letter, before
the whole and entire sense of it came home to
her understanding. The shock of hearing of the
death, under such pitiful circumstances, of Arthur's
wife, was very great, and the mournful tragedy stood
out in terrible and bold relief from amongst the mist
and confusion which at first (for Honor's intellects
were then not in the clearest possible condition)
seemed to envelope the other portions of Arthur's
letter. But very soon—*too* soon for the unhappy
woman to whom the clearing up of the mystery
seemed almost the signal for despair—light dawned
upon her bewildered mind, and with a cry of
agony, she accused herself aloud as the wretched
cause of the young mother's untimely end. At
that moment, in the first keen torture of her
self-reproach, she would have hailed as an act of
mercy from on high the relief which death, her
own death, would have brought to her. Flinging
herself on her knees beside the bed, and burying

her face in its covering, she strove, but strove in
vain, to stifle the violent hysterical sobs that *would*,
in spite of all her efforts, force themselves from
her ice-cold lips. Ah, Heaven! so the poor tor-
tured creature asked herself, how *could* she bear
the life that was before her—the life burdened with
such a dreadful, dreadful weight of guilt? Verily,
to use the concluding words of Arthur's letter,
her punishment seemed greater than she could
bear—greater by far, in one respect, than that
which had overtaken *him;* for while her fellow-
culprit could take comfort from the thought that he
might have (yet had not) sinned more heavily,
she in her despairing humility exaggerated her
guilt, and sorrowed as one that had no hope.

Life, as has been said a thousand times, is
made up of contrasts—healthy, invigorating contrasts sometimes—contrasts which, while they often
jar upon the feelings, and even sometimes tinge
with a faint and humiliating colouring of ridicule
the "situations" which they mar, are, nevertheless, as I said before, highly useful in their way,
acting as a mental *douche,* the benefit of which
may be as lasting as it is immediate. It was
such a shock as this, a trifling one in appearance,
yet not altogether without its use, that roused
Honor from the kind of trance of despair into

which she had fallen. The sound of Mrs. Casey's
voice, and the commonplace inquiry of " Please,
miss, is there anything partiklar that you'd like
for dinner?" smote upon Honor's ear like a summons from a world that she had left, and in the
interests of which she had ceased to have a share.
But although this *was* the case, and albeit her
grief and repentance were as deep and scarcely
less agonising than they had been at first, the
necessity of rising from her knees, of hiding
the traces of her agitation, and, more than all,
the obligation under which she lay, both of re-
plying to Mrs. Casey's well-meant inquiries, and
of baffling as best she might that investigating
person's very natural curiosity, all these things
were, to a certain extent, good for Honor. That
they were beneficial was evidenced by the fact that,
after Mrs. Casey had, with a very dissatisfied look,
which increased the always somewhat repulsive expression of her face, left her lodger to herself, that,
to the landlady's thinking, very mysterious and
unsatisfactory young person felt far more equal
than she had done ten minutes before to the task
of thinking, with some degree of calmness and
common sense, not only on the difficulties and
necessities of her present position, but on what
manner it had become her duty at this crisis of her
affairs to act.

Perhaps the strongest feeling (next to her own bitter self-reproach) which she was conscious of entertaining was one of deep compassion for, and sympathy with poor John's wholly undeserved sorrows. All that had passed, and the deeds which had led with such fearful rapidity to fatal and irretrievable results, appeared in all their miserable distinctness to Honor's mind. She could understand now that John, in his eagerness to discover her whereabouts, had found his way to the house where Arthur lived; and that, then and there, worked up to unjust suspicion by his mother's hints and accusations, he had with the vehemence of unbridled passion uttered the words which, overheard by Arthur's wife, had proved a death-blow to that ill-fated woman. How deeply and how lastingly the remorse of such a deed (all-unintentional though it was) would crush down the spirit of one of whose tenderness of heart Honor had had abundant proofs, she did not need in that unhappy hour to be reminded; while to act to the best of her ability the part of comforter, to strive with all the means in her power to obtain her pardon, and to induce her husband to *believe* her, and to forget the past, were now the dearest wishes of her heart. But would he —ah! there lay the *one* terrible and ever-recurring thought—would he, even after he had read the

letters which " poor" Arthur, with what Honor was
still weak enough to style his " unselfish kindness"
—had returned to her—credit the truth that her
worst faults were those of folly, of vanity; her
most unpardonable errors those arising from a
quick and rebellious temper? If she could but
see him, Honor sometimes told herself, it would
not be *very* difficult—in defiance of his mother—
to make John judge her rightfully; but though
in her more sanguine moments this was the poor
girl's persuasion, there were other, and far more
frequent occasions when she despaired of forgiveness, and when a dread of even a chance
meeting with her husband made her heart sink
within her for fear.

In this miserable fashion, alternating between
hope and depression, haunted by night as well as
by day with the memory of the dead, and with her
heart made every hour sorer by thinking on the
living, four more painful days and nights sped by.

She had been more than a week an inmate of
Mrs. Casey's house, when that thrifty personage
—who had not yet, as she elegantly termed it,
" seen the colour of Miss Blake's money"—made
her usual afternoon *entrée* into her lodger's sitting-room, with an ominous long-shaped piece of
bluish-white paper in her hand. Mrs. Casey—
whose wits were, like those of many others of

her class and kind sharpened by the instincts of
self-preservation necessary for her calling—was
surprised on her entrance by a change in her
lodger's countenance and manner, for which, seeing that Miss Blake had to the best of her belief,
received neither visitor nor letter, the worthy
landlady could by no means account. There was
a feverish flush; a light which, though it was
scarcely joy, was wonderfully revivifying in that
beautiful face; and Mrs. Casey, who had entered
the room with one of the least tender of human
purposes, felt even *her* prosaic fancy warm beneath its softening influence. Nor was the woman's surprise concerning her mysterious tenant
lessened when the latter said with a faint blush,
and hurriedly:

"Mrs. Casey, I was going to ask for you; ah,
that is your bill; and," glancing at it slightly,
"perhaps you will help me to pack up my few
things, for *I am going home!*"

She said the words, there was no mistaking
that, exultingly; and Mrs. Casey (wondering
greatly, for had not this to the end mysterious
young person told her that she had *no* home?)
uttered what was intended to be a civil congratu-
lation on this apparently altered condition in her
affairs. But Honor heard her not. With a nervous eagerness which permitted of no pause either

for thought or speech, she continued the few and
simple preparations for her departure. Drawing
forth her purse, she paid, with an absence of all
prudence, and a degree of submission to exorbi-
tant charges which caused Mrs. Casey bitterly to
regret her own moderation, the "little account"
which that lady obsequiously handed to her, and,
when all was ready, she shook hands nervously
with the woman with whom one of the thousand
chances of life had made her acquainted, and
whom she was never likely, on this side the grave,
to meet again.

"I wish you good-day, miss, and a pleasant
journey," Mrs. Casey said, taking her last inquisi-
torial survey of her late lodger through the open
window of the cab which had been summoned to
convey "Miss Blake" to the station—"and if you
should know any friends, gentlemen preferred, who
want a quiet lodging, good attendance, and everything found, perhaps you'd be good enough to
think of No. 29."

"Indeed I will," said Honour, answering the
request, as such questions usually are answered,
at random; and in another moment the owner of the
dirty net-cap and incipient moustache returned, the
impersonation of baffled curiosity, into the under-
ground precincts of the "quiet lodging," while
Honor, Hope having at last come out conqueror

over Fear, pursued her way—a thousand conflict-
ing feelings surging in her breast—towards *home!*
Home at last, home again, for all that in her husband's house Honor expected still to find the unloving woman who had once made that home so hard
to bear. Home again, though John's anger might
still be hot against her, and though she had her
pardon yet to seek. Home once more; for on that
never-to-be-forgotten day Honor had discovered
that which changed for her, in some mysterious
way, the entire aspect of her life, had made sure of
that which she fondly hoped would not only make
her peace with John, but would perhaps even
soften his mother's stony heart towards her.

"They can never, never be hard upon me *now*,"
she kept repeating to herself as visions of a great joy
yet to come, a joy that would gild over the dark and
mournful outlines of the past, rose up before her.
Visions they were of a fair child—the peacemaker
—a child with tender limbs, rounded and soft,
whose little cheek was pressed to hers, John all
the while looking at them both, the child and her,
in wonder and in love.

But, unfortunately for the sustainment of
poor Honor's courage, other and less agreeable
thoughts and anticipations took their place as she
drew nearer and more near to the home that she
was gilding with her own fancy's rays. At a dis-

tance, and buoyed up by the inward consciousness
that, in her humble way, she was blessed among
women, it had seemed no such hard matter to fall
at honest John's feet and cry, " Husband, I have
sinned before thee, and am no more worthy—inas-
much as I have been proud, passionate, and un-
grateful — to be called thy wife:" but as the
moment for confession approached, stern reality
usurped the place of fancy, and the task grew to
her thinking very hard indeed to perform. Nor
was it rendered easier by the reception—real or
imaginary—which awaited her at Switcham—
Switcham, where, a twelvemonth before, at that
self-same hour, she had returned from her bridal
tour in happiness and half in triumph, to her home,
and where, now a disgraced and lonely wanderer,
she had to endure as best she might cold looks and
disrespectful stares, from the sight of which she
escaped with eager haste into the first closed carriage that she found in waiting.

It was then that in dread and trembling she
began to repent of the impetuous haste with which
she had acted—then that she regretted her folly
in not having prepared the way for her return by
writing all she had to say to John ; for of course,
so she whispered sadly to herself, she was despised and utterly condemned. Public opinion, she
could not doubt, was against her, for John was

beloved and respected by all; while she—well, what, she asked herself, had *she* done to deserve one single emotion of affection or esteem? Nothing—to her awakened conscience told her—absolutely nothing. She had held herself aloof from her neighbours with a pride which she now knew was both mean and wicked; and she had crowned all by bringing disgrace and sorrow on the man who, from his youth upwards, had lived as a friend amongst his neighbours, gaining by his good deeds, his honesty and kindliness, the hearts of all who knew and understood his worth.

The short half-hour requisite to traverse the up-hill road that lay between Switcham and Pear-tree House sped away with cruel rapidity for Honor, who would gladly—to postpone the now dreaded moment of arrival—have deserted the lumbering "fly," which that well-known old gray mare dragged on so wearily, and, resting by the wayside, have striven better to prepare herself for the coming trial.

A cowardly wish it was, and senseless as it was cowardly, for what change, what power to endure, what gift of boldness, would time or thought bestow on one who for so many days and nights of solitary thought had been picturing to herself the meeting that was now so near at hand—the meeting which only the courage lent her by her newly-born hopes could, she now felt, enable her to support?

As each well-remembered object, while drifting with terrible rapidity towards the home she had so recklessly abandoned, met her eyes, the nervous tremor which had begun, from the moment when she neared the Switcham station, to oppress her, became gradually more difficult of control. The hour, the season, the soft evening air, the bright green of the opening leaves, the thousand tokens of the blithesome spring, all these, instead of cheering and supporting Honor's sinking spirits, lessened through the touching of some tender chord of memory, some link connected with the happy Past, her feeble powers of self-control.

When the carriage from the Dragon drew up before the woodbine-covered porch, Honor's agitation had arrived at its highest pitch, and when, at the sound of wheels upon the gravel, Hannah made her appearance at the door, and uttered, at the unexpected sight of the "young missus," a half-suppressed exclamation of astonishment, there came no sound from Honor's lips, while her feet, so incapable was she of movement, seemed glued to the time-worn sheepskin on which they rested.

With noiseless fingers—Hannah was usually a bustling servant, and the strange quiet of her

movements, together with a peculiar and unwonted stillness that reigned through the house,
filled Honor's mind with a great, but undefined,
uneasiness—with noiseless fingers then the old servant opened the door of the vehicle, and in a low,
boding whisper, her face close to Honor's ear, said
pityingly :

"Keep a good heart, dear; he ain't worse,
thank God; and the doctors, they *do* say—"

But Honor waited to hear no more. The
force of *reality*, the call for immediate action, suddenly loosened her tongue and rendered her limbs
pliant. In a moment she was by Hannah's side,
and saying in tones, unconsciously imitative of
those which had been so full of startling meaning:

"O, Hannah! what is it? O, Heaven!
he is not ill! Tell me he is not ill!" and she
strove to steady herself by clinging convulsively to
the old servant's arm.

"Hush, my dear, hush! You mustn't take on
so. I thought you'd a' known that master was
lying in the fever, or you wouldn't, maybe, be here.
But come in, there's a dear. This is the fifth day,
and Doctor Kempshall says there'll be a chrisus, I
think he calls it, soon, but whether for life or
death, the God that rules us only knows."

Hannah, who was a pious woman, and one
who held to the belief that no misfortunes happen

to us by the power that is lightly called *chance*, spoke the last words with almost devotional earnestness, adding thereby to the wild alarm that Honor was beginning to entertain.

"In danger!" she cried, "and I never knew it! O, John, dear John!" and she was hurrying to the stairs, when another step treading still more softly, and a voice more whisperingly low than even Hannah's, checked her progress.

"You musn't go, *my dear*," said Mrs. Beacham, for she it was who, looking like the ghost of her former self, pressed Honor's white cheek to hers. "You must not see John now. The fever may, the doctors say, be infectious, and if it please God to spare his life, why—" with a very sad smile, but one that was meant to be reassuring—"we may want you yet."

This reception, and the unlooked-for kindness of the broken-down old woman, was too much for Honor. Falling on her knees, and with a feeble cry of, "Forgive me! O forgive me!" she buried her face in her mother-in-law's gown, and sobbed as if her heart would break.

CHAPTER XXIV.

THE USES OF ADVERSITY.

Two more days and nights sped by — a time passed almost literally by Honor in tears and fasting — when the anxiously-looked-for crisis came at last; came in fear, and passed away in tearful hope, and the joyful news went forth that John Beacham was out of danger. Out of danger, and certain (humanly speaking) to walk forth again amongst his fellows; certain too—ay, of that there could be no doubt—that his duty to God and to his neighbours would be, to the best of his powers, as simply and faithfully performed by this honest, simple-hearted man as it had been in the days before sorrow came, and shame had visited his house. Shame, but not guilt. Ah, in that lay John's best consolation, when, with his head a little lower than had been his wont, he for the first time, with languid step and sadly altered face, sauntered in his garden between the lines of fragrant roses, leaning upon Honor's arm.

They were serious, as well as sad, those two, between whom there had been so perfect a reconciliation, and on one side a forgiveness so entire and unqualified. Honor's sweet young face looked older, paler, and far more thoughtful than of yore. She could not forget, neither could the chastened man beside her, that through *their* faults tribula-lation had fallen upon the innocent, and that a motherless infant, a bereaved father, were left to bear witness to the terrible fact that they had failed, grievously failed, in their duty to God and to their neighbour. Through all their lives the memory of these calamities would darken their joys, and cast a cloud even while the sun shone brightest, and the sky was bluest above their heads. Never again would Honor be the bright, light-hearted girl who had first won John's love when she played with the merry children in the woods, laughing and shouting in their joyous mirth. Never again would he, secure in his home happiness, and with a conscience not only void of offence towards God and towards man, but with a heart unburdened by a sense of wrong done to any soul that lived, wear upon his kindly face the genial smile which gladdened his many acquaintances, men as well as women, young as well as old, when he waved them a cordial greeting on his onward way. The zest, the freshness which

THE USES OF ADVERSITY.

makes life a thing to be enjoyed as well as endured, was over for ever; over, not only for the
man verging on middle-age, but for the woman
who, on the very threshold of existence, had
looked out on coming storms, and had learned to
dread the distant warning of the tempest.

But if not happy—happy, that is to say, with
the bliss which, like the joys of childhood, is simply
the result of ignorance, and sometimes the consequence of want of feeling or want of sense—there
were yet sufficient elements of happiness remaining
in John Beacham's home for hope to crop out
greenly from the arid sands of past regret. Not
yet had the time, the dreary time when no pleasure is taken in any created thing, arrived for them;
not yet had the hour struck when in the voice of
Nature there is no joyful sound, when the opening
spring, the song of birds, the murmur of the rippling water, appeal to the heart in vain, and when
the man who has striven through life to do his
duty, and has failed to reap the reward of peace
and the fruition of content, tells himself, in bitterness of spirit, that from the first step in life he had
chosen the wrong path, and whispers sadly to his
heart that it is all too late, alas, to retrace his
steps.

" He writes very unhappily, John," Honor was
saying. Her husband had a letter that they had

been reading in his hand—a letter to John from Arthur Vavasour. It was the second that they had received from him; the first having been one so touchingly penitent that John Beacham for a long while after reading it was more than usually silent, keeping its contents to himself, and not alluding afterwards, in any way whatsoever, to the young man's letter. But, if possible, he was after receiving it still more tender to Honor than he had been before; watching her, as she flitted about his sick-room, with eyes that glistened as they looked on her.

As soon as he was equal to the exertion, John answered the humble letter, which, coming as it did from the son of one whose memory was very dear to him, and whose good works were embalmed with the myrrh, aloes, and cassia of deep respect in the righteous man's heart, gave deep and sincere pain to its recipient; and in his reply to the penitent effusion poor John took, as such an unselfish man was certain to do, a great portion of the blame, the guilt indeed, of all that had occurred upon himself. Had a stranger read John's simple letter, he would very naturally have believed that the writer was guilty of other and worse offences than that of an impulsive yielding to first impressions, and of speaking hasty words with his tongue.

"I shall never forgive myself," he wrote. "I was a brute and a fool, and don't deserve the hap-

piness of having *my* poor wife at home with me.
Would to God, dear Mr. Arthur, that any prayers
of mine and Honor's could bring back *yours;* but
it was God's will that she should be taken, poor
young lady; but I don't understand how you
can make things better by leaving your little one
as well. I hope you will excuse my advising you;
but I loved your father well, dear Mr. Arthur, as
you know; and it grieves me to think that his son
is going into banishment like for my fault. Surely
the old gentleman would be best pleased for you
to stay at home; and besides, from all that I can
hear, America is not the best place for a young
gentleman to live in. The young ladies, too, at the
Castle would find it hard to lose you; and I should
be always remembering, seeing your empty place
at church, that it was me that was the cause you
went. No, no, dear Mr. Arthur, you will think
better of it still, I hope; and we shall see you
riding with the young ladies about the Chace this
summer, not exactly as if nothing had happened—
for that could not be, even if it was right—but as
your late lamented father would approve of, and
as your ancestors did before you. I hope that you
will be so good as excuse my boldness, and will
believe me, with respect and affection,

"Your obedient servant,

"JOHN BEACHAM."

"P.S. There is one of the beautifullest foals ever dropped, out of Mad Flora by the Old Shekarry, in the five-bar paddock. I should like you to see her, so I should. You'd say you never saw a neater nor a cleaner made one. The stock is good, and no mistake."

This letter—a letter written from the fulness of a kind and sympathising heart—found Arthur Vavasour at Liverpool, to which city he had resorted for the purpose of taking steam to the great republic—the land of *soi-disant* liberty— the land of the "stars and stripes," "unwhipped and unwhippable for ever." (I wonder, writing of that self-same flag, that some zealous descendant of the Pilgrim Fathers—some red-hot Yankee, friend and supporter of his black-bodied brethren —has not ere this voted for the suppression of the ruled, gingham-suggestive portion of the "glorious flag," for now that the negro back is free from suffering, and the weary "son of Afric" need no longer toil, the stripes would seem, one might suppose, a worse than unnecessary, because a painful, reminder of the disgraceful past.) But to return to Arthur Vavasour in the half-Americanised city, and in the big hotel to which the love of the turtle has drawn many a man who, like me and, perhaps, you, O gentle reader, has no thought whatever of crossing the broad Atlantic in a Cunard steamer. Had those afflicted ones, who so deeply commiserated the forlorn lot of this poor widower, been enabled at that moment (Asmodeus-like) to look upon his saddened face, and form their own opinions, unbiassed either by prejudice or pity, they could hardly have decided that the events of the past month had told very severely upon this young British Sybarite. At twenty-two it is very easy to forget, and with the world (a considerable portion of it, that is to say) untried and unexplored before him, a young man of good birth, the eventual possessor of such an estate as Gillingham (for even Lady Millicent could not prevent the family property from descending after her death to her eldest son)—with, I repeat, such prospects as these, to say nothing of good health and a handsome person, it is hardly surprising that Arthur Vavasour should have felt very far from utterly cast down by the changes and chances of this mortal life, of which he had lately had such painful as well as mortifying experience. He was not alone, for, seated by the open window in a rocking-chair, and reading the last number of the *Field*, then a new publication, sat a young man whose name was Godfrey Tremlett, and who, having been a college friend —the *fidus Achates* of his semi-boyish days—had

kindly consented to share the wanderings of the
disappointed man in the lands beyond the sea,
where the heavy foot of the buffalo tramples the
silent prairie, and where, flying slowly but surely
before civilisation, the red Indian (baptised with
the baptism of the Christian's "fire-water") en-
dures his lot with patience, looking, with stolid
face and all a wild man's stupid singleness of heart,
to a better, that is, a more sporting country in the
happy hunting-grounds where a good savage meets
his due reward; in other words, Arthur and his
companion's point was Fort Jasper, and their intentions were to witch the world at home with
accounts of their adventures, with details of their
narrow escapes, and with the counting over daily
of the head of game which they with their bow
and spear had bagged.

It was exciting work that talking over their
plans, examining maps of the country (rather
vague ones, it is true, but not on that account the
less interesting to the travellers), and slaying in
anticipation countless numbers of harmless animals then roaming unsuspectingly over their
native wilds.

Mr. Godfrey Tremlett was a rather heavily-
built young man, fresh-complexioned, with a fat,
beardless, good-humoured face. His appearance
was not precisely that of a sportsman; indeed, that

very morning, when he had tried on a certain hunting-suit, very short in the skirts and slightly eccentric in fashion (he had invented it himself, and took much credit to himself for the idea), Arthur, forgetful for the moment of his recent affliction, went off into roars of laughter at the singularity of his friend's appearance. Neither abashed nor affronted by this proof of intimacy, Godfrey spun round before the glass in an *accès* of self-satisfaction, which no friendly ridicule had power to check. He was essentially and invariably good-tempered. His high spirits were proof against the normal ills, the daily worries, the hourly *contretemps* of existence. He had no taste for what is generally called society. Ladies, as a rule, he considered a bore, and "fine ladies" he held in absolute, nay almost physical, dread and horror. He was not extravagant; on the contrary, he made the most of a small patrimony which had descended to him from his deceased father, and contrived to save yearly out of an income of something less than five hundred per annum a sufficient sum to enable him to enjoy in some sporting-fields or other—in Scotland, Norway, or wherever the fancy led him—a few months of excitement and variety.

To Mr. Godfrey Tremlett the idea of accompanying such a "real good fellow" as Arthur

Vavasour in the search of the latter after change and a forgetfulness of his troubles was simply delightful. He pitied his poor friend immensely, and did not at all intend that Arthur should give way to the low spirits which are generally supposed to be incidental to his situation. Neither, it must be owned, did the young widower himself betray any signs that the task of consolation would be either an impossible or a difficult one. Already change of scene, of projects, and of mode of life had produced their normal effects (as regards the young, at least) on Arthur Vavasour; and, judging by his frequent laugh, the zest with which he entered into the arrangements for his approaching campaign, and, more than all, his evident enjoyment of the good things that were set before him (namely, the *calipash* and *calipee*, which were pronounced by these two young *gourmands* to be as the nectar and ambrosia of the gods), it would have been easy for the least observant of lookers-on to convince himself that the affliction with which (for his own selfishness, his own want of moral principle, his own vanity and folly) Arthur Vavasour had been visited was but for a season, and only lightly felt by this voluntary exile.

"He does not recover his spirits," Honor said to her husband, after reading the short farewell letter in which Arthur had recapitulated his reasons for leaving England, and had dwelt in touching terms on his loneliness and his repentance. They little thought, that husband and wife, whose peace had been blighted, and whose mutual confidence shaken, if not destroyed, by this man's indulgence in vile and selfish passions, how little call there really existed in this case for compassion, and how easy it had been for Arthur Vavasour to feign a sorrow he had ceased to feel.

But while the man who had been the chief cause (humanly speaking) of this one amongst the thousand tragedies wrought by human selfishness and frailty bore his burden with such a light and unreflecting spirit, the chief sufferer by the calamity was he who was in no way—as far, that is, as short-sighted mortal eyes can see— deserving of punishment. The grief of poor Sophy's bereaved father was *for life*. For him, for the aged man, who could no longer look to new ties, new hopes to bind him to this earthly tabernacle, the loss of his child was a blow from the effects of which he never could recover. He was a Christian in thought as well as in outward belief and conduct, and he strove earnestly not only *to forgive*, but to manifest the forgiveness which he tried, not with entire success, to feel not only towards Arthur Vavasour, but towards the beautiful woman whom he ever considered, with the tenacity of faith that is characteristic of old age, as the fellow-culprit of poor Sophy's faithless husband. It is a hard thing even for the young to have their belief in all human excellence, in all human honesty, destroyed; but it is harder still upon the old, when faith and trust, the *virginities of the soul*, are for ever taken away, and when in loneliness of heart, with mistrust and suspicion usurping the place of former confidence and unquestioning credulity, they wend their weary way towards the grave in silence and in gloom. Nor was that unhappy father the only one who, mourning for the child who would not return to him, became a changed and saddened character. Mrs. Beacham, though, as might have been supposed, rather too old to learn, had yet, during the anxious days and nights when John lay between life and death, laid her shortcomings to heart, and, making some allowance for a stiff-neckedness, which had become a chronic evil of her idiosyncrasy, had reviewed the past without a certain proper sense of her own sins regarding her daughter-in-law. To confess those sins was more than could be expected of one who had arrived at the age of seventy with the conviction that all she said and did was right, beyond the possibility of question; but Mrs.

Beacham did endeavour, as much as in her lay, to make amends for the past; and although she could not wholly overcome her former jealousy of Honor's influence over her son, she kept her temper in tolerable subjection, and instead of (as was the case with Arthur) throwing the occurrences of the painful past into the waste-basket of memory, she—it was the woman's nature so to do—kept them alive with persevering industry in her breast, knowing well that with forgetfulness might come a relaxation of her constant efforts to obliterate the evil she had wrought— evil to the son she loved, and to the woman with whom, come what come might, the happiness of his future life was bound up.

Happily, both for the peace—such peace as they could henceforth hope for—of John Beacham and his wife, the little world of Sandyshire remained in ignorance of the main facts attendant on the death of young Mrs. Vavasour. She had died in childbed it was reported, and unhappily such deaths are of too common occurrence for especial wonder to be created thereby. Any reports of a close connection between John Beacham's domestic affairs and those of Arthur Vavasour and his dead wife were put a stop to by Honor's return, and by the restored affection and trust which, after John's recovery, were seen to exist, not only between the husband and wife, but between Honor and her hitherto implacable mother-in-law. They left the Paddocks for a time, a few not unhappy weeks, change of air and scene having been recommended by the doctors for the perfecting of John's recovery; and during that absence from their home the bonds of affection, strengthened by the ties of a great sorrow shared between them, were knit very closely together. The dawn of their wedded life had been overcast with clouds; the morning had been dull, and doubts of whether fine weather would even come at noon had strengthened as the day grew older. But the "morning gray," according to the old shepherd's adage, will not, let us hope, fail to end in the "fine day" that ofttimes follows. The grieving over love's decay is of all griefs the gloomiest. To be shedding—I speak of a wife now (men's eyes are not formed for weeping)—to be shedding secret tears over the memory of an affection passed away is a very hopeless form of sorrow. The

" Distilling bitter, bitter drops
From sweets of former years"

formed, however, no part of the trials to which Honor Beacham was henceforth exposed. *Her* duty was, by undying efforts to efface the memory of past error, and to strive by every act and word

to render herself worthy of a good man's love.
The memory of the bitter past—of the past, uncon-
nected by any lack of love on John's part—could
never, never be washed away; but to "redeem
the time," the present that was left to her, became,
because of the evil of the days that were past,
a still more sacred duty.   Sorrow had done good
service in forming while it humbled the character
of our poor little impulsive heroine, for "la vertù
è simile ai perfumi, che rendono più grato odore
quando-riturati."   Heaviness had indeed endured
for the morning, but content, if not joy, had come
to her and hers with the quiet evening light.

CONCLUSION.

IF the reader of this half-true story has followed with any portion of just indignation the tortuous ways through which an insane craving after power has lead the nominal heroine of these pages, he or she will not regret to learn that, in consequence of a high legal opinion—*the* highest, indeed, in the land—having been given, at the eleventh hour, against the possibility of setting aside Earl Gillingham's last will and testament, Lady Millicent was forced, with a reluctance comparable only to the pang of plucking out a right eye or wrenching out a wrong tooth, to abandon the unfilial as well as unmotherly intention which she had so long secretly as well as avowedly harboured.

The intense though silent wrath of Lady Millicent when she found that the great law-lords were not to be led—albeit the forceps or chain, call it what you will, was held and drawn by a lady of great estate, strong courage, and ancient name—entirely by the nose may be better imagined than described. Misfortunes never, according to the old adage, come singly, and this autocratic lady found the proof of the proverb to her cost. In her youth she had never cared to provide herself with friends, and, when it was too late, she made the unwelcome discovery that there are certain manufactures of which the art cannot be learned save in the freshness and elasticity of early womanhood. The world, too, which had interested itself a good deal in Lady Millicent's efforts, and which was hesitating as to its decision from a laudable desire to side with the strongest, bore rather hardly in her discomfiture on the baffled and indignant woman. That she had been unmotherly, grasping, avaricious—everything that was least feminine and most odious—everyone was more than willing to allow; whereas Arthur—regarding whom heads had been ominously shaken, and of whose scampishness so many (while the great affair was in abeyance) had a word, more or less severe, to say—became once more the popular " young fellow," the idol of fair women's hearts, and the object of future attacks from prudent mammas and half-despairing *demoiselles à marier.*

It was while smarting under the first wounds inflicted by disappointed ambition and frustrated love of power that Lady Millicent discovered the bitter truth that as we sow so we must reap, and

that there can be no harvest of affection where
the seeds of tenderness have been neglected to
be sown. The news—very melancholy intelligence
it was to his brother and his sisters—that Arthur
Vavasour had, for an indefinite period, bade farewell to home and country, child and kindred,
was communicated to Lady Millicent by her son
Horace. He, the younger brother, who had always been in secret very impatient of parental
control, and whose strong affection for his elder
brother had ever been a marked and amiable feature of his character, was roused by the departure
of Arthur to the strongest feelings of displeasure
against the mother whose unfeeling conduct had,
in his opinion, been the cause of her son's expa-
triation. Walking one morning unannounced into
the dull morning-room in which Lady Millicent,
now that the occupation of her life was over, sat
brooding over the turpitude and cowardice of lawyers, and the general injustice and stupidity of all
connected with wills and will-making, Horace Vavasour took the liberty of giving his mother a
piece of his mind.

"So, ma'am," he began, his lips pale with
agitation, and his voice (Horace was a little shaken
by a year's dissipation) a trifle difficult to steady,
—" so, ma'am, Arthur's off—gone—bolted. This
confounded law-business put the finishing-stroke

to his affairs, poor fellow! I knew how it would be. He never had a chance of doing well—never, by G—!" and Horace, who was standing near some greenhouse plants in full flower, whirled his light riding-whip lasso-like over their heads, thereby ruthlessly severing some half-dozen from their parent stems.

Lady Millicent looked up in mute dismay. The outbreak was so unexpected, and disrespect to her person and authority an occurrence so entirely new, that for a moment she found no words either sufficiently powerful or cutting for the expression of her indignation. At last she said, drawing herself up haughtily:

"You forget yourself strangely. What have I to do with Arthur's—with your brother's—eccentricities? Gone, is he? And where, pray? On some self-indulgent freak or other, I suppose, to escape the sight of that poor old man's miserable face; but what this 'law-business,' as you call it, has to do with the matter, is more than I either understand, or wish to have explained."

She rose from the sofa as she spoke, but was arrested by her son's hand laid lightly on her shoulder.

"Mother," he said almost sternly, "for once in my life I will speak to you openly. It will

be the first time and the last; for you are not one,
or I am greatly mistaken, to forgive the words that
I shall use. From our childhood you never, *never*
treated us as if you loved us. As a little fellow,
so little, I remember, that I could scarcely reach
the table with my hand—as a small boy—troublesome, I daresay, as all young children are, but not
more depraved and wicked than others—I longed
—O, *how* I used to long!—for love and tenderness
from you. When I saw other mothers kiss and
pet their children, holding them upon their knees,
and looking with delight and pride upon their
play and laughter, I can never describe to you
the bitter envy that I felt, and with what a sore,
sad heart I thought upon the difference between
them and me! And it was the same with all of
us. We have compared notes many times since
those days, and have told each other—we four
children, whom my father left a legacy to you; ah,
shall I ever forget his dying words?—that we only
wanted love, only the common tenderness shown
by all God's creatures to their young, and that,
having it, we would return it fifty, ay, a hundred-
fold! But—and well you know it, mother—we
had it not, that love we yearned for; and failing
the boon we craved, we all went"—and he smiled
bitterly—" more or less, and in different ways, according to our respective powers and sexes, to the

bad. There is Arthur, poor dear Atty," and his lip quivered painfully, "gone, without a word—excepting that he confessed some things to that poor broken-hearted old man which would make your cheek, ma'am, grow red with shame, although you love him not, to hear of. It seems, he was reduced—I and some others think that the fault was not *quite* all his own—to do some ugly thing which, but for the law-business of which you speak so lightly, need never have been known, and—"

"Ah, I understand," put in Lady Millicent, endeavouring to hide her confusion and annoyance under a mask of carelessness and sarcasm. "Difficulties in the way of raising money, eh? But that is over now," she added bitterly, "and I suppose that your brother need not, as matters now stand, fly the country because he does not happen to be able to pay his bills."

"No, ma'am, you are right there," rejoined her son; "but, unfortunately, poor Arthur, almost maddened by grief and worry, and believing, as so many did, that the 'high legal opinion' (on which depended your continuance or otherwise in the disputing of my grandfather's will) would be, when given, adverse to his interests, had not moral courage, or rather his pecuniary embarrassments were too great to admit of any longer delay; so he has gone, poor dear fellow." And

Horace drew a long troubled breath, for, like many others, he believed in the reality as well as the endurance of Arthur's grief. "He has gone away, poor old boy, for years, he says; and—and old Dub told me this morning that Arthur was—a villain!"

He was very young, that warm-hearted Horace, whose admiration of and love for his elder brother had truly grown with his growth and strengthened with his strength. For a long hour that morning he had stoutly fought Arthur's battles with the old man, who, embittered by misfortune, and rendered thereby callous to the feelings of others, had dilated in no measured terms on his son-in-law's utter want of principle, his selfishness, his mendacity, and his general and irretrievable unworthiness. It was in vain that Horace endeavoured to convince the obstinate and sorely-tried millionaire — the wealthy merchant-prince, whose gold had been unavailing to purchase an hour of life for the child of his old age—that Arthur's offences were less dark than they appeared, and that excuses might, if sought for *with a will*, be found even for this self-exiled sinner. To all the arguments, all the recapitulations of the affectionate brother tending to throw a light on the manifest disadvantages attendant on poor Arthur's "raising," "old Dub" would only shake his gray head with the mournfullest of dismal gestures, and with a "Well, well," which betokened alike a weariness of spirit and an absence of conviction that irritated Horace, while filling his heart with a pity beyond the reach of words.

He was very young, as I before said, or not only would these things not have taken such a strong effect upon his temper and his mind, but it may be that, after the utterance of the last terrible word, he would not — an act which he was weak enough to commit — have flung himself upon a lounging-chair near him, and, burying his face in his hands, have striven hard, yet ineffectually, to conceal his emotion.

Lady Millicent meanwhile looked on in silence; but, although apparently unmoved, she was, perhaps, nearer to giving way to a burst of sorrow than she had ever been in all her life before. It had, indeed, been a shock to her to learn that one of the ugliest of accusing words had been applied by a person on whom she looked down as the dust beneath her feet, to son of hers. The sight, also, of Horace—his face buried in his hands, and the tears trickling between his clenched fingers—acted, if not upon her heart, upon her nerves; and even as the melting of the winter's snow tears up the stones most deeply buried in the torrent's bed, Lady Millicent, moved by those hard-wrung drops

to pity and to grief, could, had she yielded to one
of the best and purest impulses she had ever
known, have fallen on her son's neck and wept
aloud.

For everything—turn which way she would,
to the right hand or the left—everything at which
she looked, whether in the past, the present, or
the future, seemed against the unhappy woman
who had so long hardened her heart and stiffened
her neck against reproof. Her children—the sons
and daughters whom, strange to say, she now, in
the days of her defeat and in the hour of her
humiliation discovered *were* of some value in her
sight—became to her as instruments of punishment. It was surprising to what extent the love
of power, and the dread of abdicating to another
the sceptre of her rule, had blinded this woman to
a sense not only of her duties, but of her affections. The hope, the aim that she had so long in
view, of still retaining within her grasp the dominion that she so dearly loved, had absorbed
every faculty, both of mind and heart; but when
that hope had vanished, and when the purpose of
her life was at an end, then—when, with the natural
yearning of every woman who still retains some
of the characteristics of her sex, for an object on
which to expend the hopes and fears, the energies
and anticipations of a still vigorous mind, she

turned with almost a passionately longing heart to the children whom God had given her—they in their turn refused the tardy boon thrown *faute de mieux* for their acceptance.

The children of Cecil Vavasour refused—tacitly, it is true, and with the firm protest of silent apathy —the offering of a mother's interest in their affairs, a parent's sympathy with their sorrows. Many a year too late there sounded, for those neglected children of a good and Christian father, the cry of nature in the breast of that world-hardened and power-loving woman. They could not—*could* not love her. Like stunted trees, blighted by long exposure to cold winds and nipping frosts, the feeble sap within had ceased to rise, and no new shoots, no tender buds of love and tenderness, had opened beneath the warmth of maternal love, even as in the joyous spring the young leaves turn towards the sun their grateful tribute.

In other words, Lady Millicent's children, albeit they did not openly either resist her authority or turn a cold shoulder to her tardy advances, were what is vulgarly called " no comfort" to her at this trying season of her life—a season when disappointment rendered still more unendurable to others a temper already none of the sweetest, and when consciousness of failure

subdued a spirit that had hitherto risen proudly
above the threatened ills of life.

Perhaps, had Lady Millicent's children been
enabled to look within the heart that had at last
begun to melt beneath the influence of maternal
tenderness, their feelings might have been softened,
moved by the knowledge that, in spite of bygone
proofs to the contrary, they were nevertheless
beloved; but no such fairy-gift being bestowed
upon them, and it being a boasted peculiarity
of Lady Millicent's idiosyncrasy that she never
betrayed to others the feelings that were making
havoc in her breast, it followed that not only the
son whose grief for his brother's departure had
first aroused her maternal sympathies, but that
the daughters—the sickly Rhoda and the more
spirited Katherine—should have remained in ignorance of their mother's yearnings after affection, while, in a silence full of reproachful meaning, they brooded over the events of the past.

Of the three who so often met together to
talk in saddened whispers of their banished brother, of poor Sophy's death, and, when Rhoda
was not present, of *her* failing health, her broken
spirits, she who was the most rebellious, the least
willing to submit to the gloom which death and
failure had cast around their home, was Kate—
Kate, the gay-hearted and the *insouciante*—Kate

who had expected to marry, and had hoped to be happy—Kate, to whom the idea of a return, *in statu quo*, to the dulness and monotony of Gillingham was as a sentence of banishment to a desert land beyond the seas. And after all they did not return, at least for the *dead* season, to Gillingham; for a medical opinion, demanded with an anxiety carefully hidden from her children, on the condition of Rhoda's health pronounced that for the *chance* of life it was absolutely necessary that before the autumn should set in Miss Vavasour must be in the sunny island where so many victims to east winds and defective lungs retire to die.

They are at Madeira now, those three sad and silent women; sad and silent, for Lady Millicent was too old to change the habits of a life, and Rhoda—depressed not only by a blighted attachment but by the sickness which is unto death—makes no effort to seem the thing she is not. Only Kate still longs and pines to be happy, but it is hard to fight against reality, and very hard to kick against the pricks. She *knows* that the fiat has gone forth, and that her poor pale Rhoda—the Rhoda who might, so Katie thinks, have been the contented wife of stupid George Wallingford — is to die. She foresees a dismal future with the mother whom she believes to be

the cause of all their various sorrows, and
Katherine's rosy face begins to lose its freshness, and her voice its joyous tone while dwelling
on the sadness of the days to come.

Reader, there is no crime related in these
volumes; no commandment has been ostensibly
and boldly broken; and yet the consequences
of hidden sins, of sins unwhipped of justice, have
proved terribly disastrous both to the "living that
now live, and to the dead that have been called
to judgment." It is not always, it is not even
often, that the results of an indulgence in evil
passions, in iniquitous desires, and in the hungering
after the things that belong neither of our own
peace nor to that of others, are brought immediately before us. It may be that while we, in
a safe haven from the storms of life at the season
when

"Age steals to its allotted nook,
Contented and serene,"

are ignorant of the fact that the errors of others
may be visited on our heads, "some forlorn and
shipwrecked brother," some poor deluded sister
may be rueing the consequences (indirectly) of our
shortcomings. Even of our very words — our
thoughtlessness and apparently unmeaning re-
marks—evil may arise. The French proverb says,

" *Oui et non sont bien courts à dire, mais avant que de les dire il y faut penser longtemps.*" Alas, how few amongst us are there who think before they *act,* how fewer still before they speak! A precious life may be lost, a child may be rendered motherless, the hearth of the old may be made desolate, and all because of thoughtless words spoken to foolish ears; while the truth of the old historian's words " Cupido dominandi cunctis affectibus flagrantior est," is to a certain degree verified by the evils which a love of power and a mean jealousy of rule have entailed upon more than one deserving character in the foregoing pages. Truly, seeing that we are but links in the great chain of human events, it behoves us to take good heed, not only to our *ways* but to the seeing that we offend not with the unruly member, which, according to high authority, never has and never can be brought under subjection. The characters in my story, whose future is darkened, and whose past has been made miserable by the great mischief which their busy tongues, their truant fancies, have wrought, can hardly (at least in the world's opinion) be stigmatised as desperate and grievous sinners. They had *only* not bridled the " little member, which boasteth great things," had only *listened* when duty should have caused them to close their ears to words which were dangerous because either too tender or too hard! Such had been amongst the sins of those whose punishment would be life-long — life-long, because for them the past is embittered by vain regrets—life-long, for neither to the mother who was false to her trust, nor to the old, the middle-aged, or the young whose faults and follies have been cited in this story, can *remorse* be divorced from the sad paths of memory — life-long because, looking back upon the stream of life, they, with heavy hearts, could not fail to see, midst the soft rippling waves, the heavy stone that

> "some devil threw
> **At their life's mid-current, thwarting God!"**

THE END.

LONDON:
ROBSON AND SON, GREAT NORTHERN PRINTING WORKS,
PANCRAS ROAD, N.W.